PINK RIBBON
The Benningtons
Book 3

ANNABELLE MARIN

Published by Blushing Books
An Imprint of
ABCD Graphics and Design, Inc.
A Virginia Corporation
977 Seminole Trail #233
Charlottesville, VA 22901

Pink Ribbon
Annabelle Marin

eBook ISBN: 978-1-63954-545-2
Print ISBN: 978-1-63954-546-9

The Bennington Family Tree

Paul Bennington (1821-1870)
Petunia Bennington (1822-1859)
Christopher Bennington (b.1840. 30 years old)
Steve Bennington (b.1842. 28 years old)
Hugh Bennington (b.1845. 25 years old)
Poppy Bennington (b.1845. 25 years old)
Anthony Bennington (b.1849. 21 years old)
Iris Bennington (b.1855. 15 years old)
Lily Bennington (b.1859. 11 years old)

Prologue

"THE PAY WON'T BE much since you are just starting out, but you will get room and board, three square meals a day, and Sundays off, along with the rest of the holidays." Seventeen-year-old Finn Weston wiggled his torn sock-covered feet inside his worn-out boots which wouldn't last another season.

They had been a faithful pair since leaving behind his pa, ma, and eleven siblings in Virginia, in search of a better future. He was a middle child surrounded by ten other boys, in a small town where there wasn't much hope for progress despite everyone's false assumptions that better days would come.

Finn cleared his throat when the awkward silence settled between them. His new boss, Christopher Bennington, was just nineteen years old but looked older due to the fact he never smiled and was quick-tempered. Despite his grimace, he'd heard Christopher was a fair boss and there weren't many places he could work in Larkspur Valley, Wyoming.

He was uneducated—he had stopped going to school

when he was twelve because his pa needed help saving their family's dying farm. His teachers had always told him he was a good student and Finn still enjoyed reading during the cold winter months, when there wasn't much to do. He also didn't know how to do much besides farm work, and his arithmetic wasn't as good as his reading.

Finn didn't care much about prestige anyhow. He just wanted to save enough money to build himself a nice home and have a wife and a couple of kids. Not eleven, though, that was too many.

"I'm not afraid of hard work, Mr. Bennington. I've been used to it all my life."

Christopher nodded as he rested his hand against his belt buckle, looking exhausted. Finn had only been in Larkspur Valley for a week, but he already knew through the grapevine that Christopher's mother had died only a few months ago after giving birth to the seventh Bennington child, Lily. The patriarch of the family had been distraught, and with a newborn to take care of, Christopher had taken over the ranch.

"Good to hear. Call me Christopher, or Chris. We are nearly the same age after all. I don't like being addressed like my father." Christopher stopped in front of a large, wooden cabin. "You'll share this cabin with six other men. You'll meet our cook, Hattie, in the morning. You'll have to take care of your own washing."

Finn nodded politely. He made a mental note to build himself his own house as soon as possible. After sharing a room with his brothers for a long time, he wanted some privacy.

After giving him a tour of the cabin and introducing him to the other men, Christopher invited him for a drink at his bachelor home. His home was smaller than the main Bennington home just a few miles away. Christopher, along with his brother, Steve, and their father had built it shortly before Mrs. Bennington died.

Finn was just finishing telling Christopher about his home in Virginia when a little blonde stormed into the parlor. She couldn't have been more than fourteen years old, with long blonde hair messily arranged with a pink ribbon.

The girl was Christopher's sister as they both shared the same stunning blue eyes. Her pink dress clung to her small, scrawny body with the front covered in spit and food. The blonde was holding a crying baby in her arms who couldn't have been more than a few months old. Finn guessed it must be the newest member of the Bennington family.

Baby Lily's face was bright red as she hollered her head off, her little fist clinging onto the girl's hair. A four-year-old girl looking adorably confused clung to her elder sister's skirts sucking on her thumb, while the ten-year-old skinny boy next to her looked embarrassed.

"Poppy," Christopher scolded his sister. "What did I tell you about barging in here?"

"You told me you would be back home at two to help me with Lily," Poppy practically screeched. "It's almost four, and I need to get dinner started and, of course, stupid Hugh and Steve decided to disappear—" She blushed when she finally noticed Finn. "Hello, good afternoon."

Finn tipped his head politely, not wanting to embarrass her. The pink ribbon fell from her hair and Finn picked it up, handing it to her. Poppy stuffed it in her pocket while Lily continued screeching. "I'm Finn Weston, miss."

"Poppy Bennington," Poppy said quietly. "This is Lily. My sister, Iris, and my brother, Anthony." Iris blushed and looked at the floor while Anthony managed a small wave. She then turned to look at Christopher. "She's been crying all morning."

The poor girl looked exhausted. It was clear she was the

one taking care of the three younger siblings since their mother passed away. She was so young and she already had all that responsibility on her shoulders instead of being able to enjoy herself like other young girls her age.

Christopher looked helpless. "It's probably colic like Mrs. Mead said. Have you tried rocking her like she suggested?"

"Nothing works!" she screeched. She was obviously too young to be taking care of three young children on her own, especially without a mother or grandmother to help her out.

"Where's Father?"

"He went to visit Mother's tomb. Iris and Anthony have been behaving, but I don't know what to do about Lily."

An awkward silence settled before Finn cleared his throat. "May I try calming her down? I have four younger brothers. I know how to soothe babies."

Poppy practically threw Lily at him. It took Finn a few minutes, but he managed to rock Lily to sleep.

Poppy sighed in relief as she rubbed her tired eyes. Anthony and Iris looked pleased. It seemed their screaming sister had tired them out as well.

Christopher ran a hand through his dark hair. "Impressive. Perhaps I should hire you as a nanny instead."

Finn laughed.

He wouldn't have minded working with children. He had practically helped his mother raise the younger ones before his father had required his help in taking care of the farm.

The young blond man looked at Poppy, who finally relaxed when she looked at her sleeping sister, the tension melting away from her shoulders. She was quite pretty and sweet when she wasn't overwhelmed with responsibilities.

Both of them were young now, but he promised himself that once he earned money, built her a home, and she was of marriageable age, he would ask her father for her hand. They would live a happy life.

Finn would make sure of it.

Chapter 1

FEBRUARY 1872, *Larkspur Valley, Wyoming…*

Breathe, just breathe, Poppy. You can do this. You just have to say the vows and you will finally be married. Twenty-seven-year-old Poppy Bennington stopped practicing her breathing when she realized it wasn't working in calming her down, despite her sister-in-law's insistence.

She stepped away from the window of her childhood bedroom to look at her reflection in her vanity mirror. Poppy expected to see wrinkles, but a smooth, pale, nervous face looked back at her. Everyone in town, including her own family, had been calling her a spinster for years, so it still surprised her at times how young she looked, especially when she was feeling vulnerable.

Her golden hair was pulled back in a smooth bun and her sister-in-law, Ruby, who was married to her brother, Steve, had added lilies in her hair. Ruby had even added something to her cheeks which caused them to bloom pink. No doubt something she had learned from her whoring days in the brothel.

It was a rare, sunny day in February. Perhaps it was a

good omen, indicating that her marriage would be a long and prosperous one.

Poppy's dress felt heavy and tight. It took all her willpower not to rip the row of buttons lining up against her neck. She suddenly wondered why she had insisted to her brothers that she needed an expensive, professionally made dress from the best dressmaker in town when Christopher's wife, Lucy, had offered to make her wedding gown.

Lucy's dress would surely have made her feel prettier. Instead, she felt like an ornate pillow rather than a pretty bride.

Poppy let out a small growl. This wasn't how she was supposed to feel on her wedding day to Richard Glass. She was supposed to feel pretty, dainty, more wife-like. She felt like a little girl playing dress up.

She wasn't sure why she was so nervous. She had been courting Richard for almost a year. He was a good man who worked at the post office. Poppy would live in town instead of the countryside and she would be able to host dinners, participate in her brother's church more, and see Iris and Lily on their way to school. Best of all, she wouldn't be known as the evil, ugly, short-tempered Bennington spinster after today.

Then why did she feel so unhappy? It was like she was trying to fit her foot into a small shoe.

She heard a loud knock on the door before her sister, thirteen-year-old Lily, came barging in wearing a pink dress with a matching straw hat and tiny white gloves, all made exclusively by her talented sister-in-law, Lucy.

"Are you almost ready, Pop? We're going to be late!" It was Lily's first wedding where she was a bridesmaid instead of the flower girl and she was obviously very excited. Seventeen-year-old Iris would be her maid of honor, even though she would rather be studying than attending a wedding.

Poppy couldn't remember if she had ever been as happy as Lily, even before her mother's death. She had always been a meek, uninteresting child who was prone to anger when things didn't go her way, while Lily was a little ray of sunshine.

"You are supposed to wait for my response before you barge it. Honestly, Lily, you are thirteen years old. You will never be a proper lady if you keep behaving like this," Poppy scolded, sounding like an elderly woman.

Lily's shoulders slumped. "I'm sorry. I just want everything to be perfect." She squeezed her hand. "Oh, Poppy, you are such a beautiful bride. I hope when I get married, I'll look just as beautiful as you."

"You will, sweetheart. You'll be even prettier. I'm sorry for being cross. I just never thought this day would happen is all."

"Are you nervous?"

"No, just a little tired. We planned the wedding in such a short time. I've hardly gotten a wink of sleep."

"Chris and Steve went ahead, to make sure everything is ready at the church and to greet the guests," Lily piped up. Unlike Christopher and Steve, who had had very intimate weddings with just the family, Richard and Poppy had invited about thirty guests from town.

"Lucy stayed behind to make sure your dress or veil didn't need any last-minute fixing and Ruby is going to carry Silver while she throws flowers. Iris is reading like she always is." Silver was Ruby and Steve's baby daughter. She was only a few months old and the cutest baby Poppy had ever seen.

"And Hugh?"

"He's waiting in the carriage and growing more impatient by the second."

"The bride is supposed to be late."

Originally, Christopher was going to walk her down the aisle, as the eldest, but she had begged Christopher to let Hugh do it. He was her fraternal twin, after all, and he had been with her since birth. Hugh understood her when no one else did.

"Do you need help with your veil?" Lily inquired.

Poppy nodded. Her hands were shaking too much. She wondered who would attend the ceremony. She had always been too busy and unfriendly to make friends, with the exception of Lucy and Ruby.

Specifically, she wondered if a certain blond rancher would attend.

"There you go, perfect." Lily smiled as she pulled back so Poppy could look at herself in the mirror. The veil had belonged to her mother. Her eyes watered with tears, suddenly wishing both of her parents were here. Perhaps then, she wouldn't feel so nervous.

"Let's go, before Hugh drags us out by the ear." Poppy forced a smile as she walked downstairs. It was strange that she would never live here again. She had been running the Bennington household since she was fourteen years old.

"Here comes the bride!" Lily practically screamed.

Iris, dressed in a matching pink dress, put down her book, Lucy stopped playing with the bow around her waist which was drawing attention to her small, pregnant belly, and baby Silver squealed in delight while Ruby tried to hold her.

Her younger sister looked impressed for once in her life, which was shocking since she didn't care about dresses or fixing her hair. "You look beautiful."

"Like a lovely princess. No, a queen!" Lucy was practically crying tears of joy. It still amazed Poppy how someone who had had such a harsh life as an orphan was so damn sensitive.

"The prettiest bride in all of Larkspur Valley," Ruby offered generously. Poppy accepted the compliment even though Ruby was one of the most beautiful women Poppy had ever seen. It was hard not to feel jealous of her at times.

Poppy's cheeks flushed red. She wasn't used to receiving so much attention and she was suddenly feeling a bit shy. "Thank you." She cleared her throat. "We should get going before my brother throws a fit."

It was no secret that Hugh preferred to be at his medical practice than walking his twin down the aisle.

Hugh was waiting impatiently in the family's large buggy which had been adorned by the girls with the few flowers they could find and white ribbons. It was terribly chilly and she wished she could wear a coat.

"You're late," her twin scolded but helped her up. "Only you would dare to get married in the coldest month of the year."

"It's the month of father's death," Poppy whispered carefully. "We needed something happy to associate this month with, instead of reminding us that we lost him so early."

Hugh's face softened slightly as he kissed her cheek. "I know, Pop. We could have picked something simpler than a wedding, though."

Poppy laughed.

Hugh helped his sisters up, then Lucy and Ruby, with Silver on her lap. Twenty-five minutes later, they were in front of the church Poppy's brother ran as the pastor. Poppy clung to the flowers nervously in her lap. She could see her guests' heads in the church even from her buggy.

Her twin checked his pocket watch and cursed. "We're late,

like expected. Iris, stand up and take Silver with you. You two are going to lead the way into the church anyway. Lily, go find Anthony, Steve, and Christopher and tell them we are here."

Lily grumbled, obviously not pleased by the order as Iris took the baby.

Hugh turned back to his sister as he helped her down. "Are you sure about this, Pop? It's not too late to change your mind."

Ruby glared at him. "Honestly, Hugh, you are making her more nervous than she already is. Look at her; she's shaking."

"I just want her to be sure, my meddling sister-in-law. Marriage is forever," Hugh quipped back.

"I'm ready," Poppy interrupted their bickering, her chin held up high. "I'm twenty-seven. I should have been married a long time ago."

Hugh didn't look like he believed her, but thankfully he didn't question her as he gave her one last kiss on the cheek before heading towards the church's entrance. "I'll be waiting at the entrance to let the three of you fuss over Poppy's dress. Two minutes, not a minute more."

As Lucy and Ruby smoothed down her skirts and rearranged her veil, Poppy's eyes went towards the church. "Do you think he's there?"

Lucy flinched.

Ruby growled. "Don't start. Finn proposed to you at least half a dozen times and you rejected him. There's no point in crying over past decisions."

Ruby's words stung, but she knew she was right. Poppy had made her bed and now she had to lie in it.

"I wouldn't feel comfortable watching the person I care for get married to someone else," Lucy said softly. "Poppy, you said yourself you didn't want to marry Finn because he's a strict disciplinarian like your brothers and you didn't want to get spanked in your marriage. Has that changed? Because if it has, then you must tell Richard—"

"No, I love Richard and we will be very happy together." Poppy straightened her spine. "Don't mind me, Lu, it's just wedding nerves. Finn and I have known each other for over ten years. I just thought he would put his pride aside and attend my wedding."

Ruby rolled her eyes. "Finn might not be as bull-headed as Steve and Christopher, but he is still a man. Of course, he cares about his pride." The blonde frowned. "What are they arguing about now?"

The three women turned to stare at the Bennington brothers, minus Anthony, who were whispering angrily a few feet away before they approached Poppy and their wives.

"What's going on?" Poppy continued to smile. "We are not that late, are we?"

The three of them exchanged dark looks before Christopher spoke up. "He's not coming. What I'm trying to say is he never showed up in the first place."

"Who?" she asked dumbly.

"What do you mean 'who?' The imbecile you agreed to marry!" Hugh snapped.

"Anthony is trying to keep the guests seated, but we can't put if off for much longer," Christopher explained calmly. "We must explain to them that there will be no wedding."

Poppy shook her head. "No, there must be a mistake. Richard will be here; he promised. Perhaps he overslept or he's getting ready. This is an important day for me. For us. He wouldn't just leave me in the cold."

Steve placed a hand on her shoulder. "Poppy, honey, I went to check his house myself when he never showed up. The house is empty. He didn't leave a note and his horse is gone. He skipped town before the wedding. I don't think he ever planned on marrying you, or if he did, something happened to change his mind."

Christopher looked at her with pity. "I am so sorry, sweetheart."

Ruby swore, causing Steve to scold her while Lucy rubbed her back.

Tears pooled in her eyes. Poppy suddenly felt terribly hot and itchy in the too-tight wedding dress. She was a jilted bride. An embarrassment. A spinster. Everyone in town would be whispering for months about how the bitter and sharp-tongued Poppy Bennington managed to scare away the third man who'd shown interest in her. She would be a laughingstock.

She would be the woman mothers warned their young daughters about. A cautionary tale.

"No, you're lying. Richard wouldn't leave me; he promised he would marry me!"

"Poppy, honey—"

"Stop lying!" she shrieked as she jumped inside the buggy and held the reins of the horses tightly. Voices around her scolded her and tried to calm her down, but she refused to listen. If Richard had truly abandoned her, she had to see it with her own eyes.

Poppy forced the horses to go forward, not letting them stop until they reached Richard's little house near the post office. Poppy jumped down, not bothering to tie the horses to the nearby pole.

She pushed the door open slowly, her white gown standing out sharply against the simple wooden furniture. Her brothers were right. Even though the furniture was there, all of his personal tokens, such as his books and trinkets, were gone. She searched the bedroom and found the same thing, not a stitch of clothing was left behind, not even a note explaining his decision.

Poppy made her way numbly back to the sitting room. The sight of the deserted place which was supposed to be her and Richard's home was too much to bear. She sank to her knees, unable to contain her tears anymore.

Loud sobs exploded out of her, staining her veil and the top of her dress. Was she so terrible? Is that why no one wanted to marry her? Was this her punishment for treating Finn so cruelly in the past?

"Oh, Pop," Hugh sighed as he kneeled down next to her. He must have run all the way from the church. "Richard is not worth your tears. I swear to you if he ever steps foot in this town again, I will tear him limb from limb and force feed him his intestines."

This only made Poppy cry harder.

Hugh sighed. "Let's go home, Pop."

When Poppy didn't move, Hugh picked her up in his arms despite her heavy wedding dress and dragged her back into the buggy. Her sisters, along with Ruby and Lucy, were waiting for her once they returned home, no doubt wanting to fuss over her.

Her brothers were nowhere to be found, and Poppy guessed they were probably at the church letting the guests know about their sister's humiliation.

"Do you want a sedative?" Hugh asked carefully as he plopped her down on the bed.

"No," Poppy answered numbly as she removed her veil. She wanted to burn it, but it had been her mother's. Perhaps Iris and Lily would have better luck than she and actually get married. "I just want to be alone."

Hugh nodded, kissing her forehead before he departed.

Lucy, Ruby, Iris, and Lily came in seconds after Hugh left. Their eyes filled with pity as they looked at the poor, sad little spinster.

Looking at them, just made the anger and resentment

she was feeling inside her chest grow. It reminded Poppy how much better their lives were. Both Ruby and Lucy were adored and loved by their husbands and were starting to form their own families. Lily and Iris were young and beautiful, with their whole lives ahead of them. They had never had to sacrifice their time and their youth to raise children after the Benningtons' matriarch had died.

They didn't understand. None of them did.

Every time Poppy was at the brink of happiness, it was taken away.

Iris was the first to speak as she shifted awkwardly in her new shoes. "How can we help you? Do you want food?"

"I want all of you to leave, please."

Lucy bit her lip. "It's not good for you to be alone. You need your family. What Richard did was unforgivable."

Ruby nodded. "We should search for him and make him pay for all of the hurt he caused you. When I was working at the brothel, one of the girls... well, I'll tell you when Lily and Iris are not present. This isn't something unmarried girls should hear."

"I want to hear!" Lily whined.

"Now, Ruby, revenge is never the answer."

"All I'm saying, Lucy, is Richard should not be forgiven for the humiliation he caused her."

"Get out." Poppy couldn't stand the bickering. She just wanted to be alone. Away from the world. Why couldn't they understand that?

"But, Poppy—"

"I said leave! Get the hell out; I don't want to see any of you right now! I don't want your pity!" Poppy threw a pillow at them that they managed to dodge, and she ended up knocking over a lamp instead. "Just leave me alone!"

Poppy ignored the hurt look in their eyes as Lily picked up the lamp. Surprisingly, it hadn't broken.

Lucy squeezed her shoulder before she turned to look at the other women with a motherly look on her face. "We should go. It's been a long day for Pop. She needs her rest."

Lily kissed her cheek. "Let us know if you need anything, Poppy. Please don't be sad. You still have us."

One by one, they started going downstairs, leaving Poppy in her childhood bedroom with the packed trunks staring back at her mockingly. Is this how it was going to be from now on? Living in her childhood bedroom, watching every one of her siblings get married while she lived on as the spinster aunt?

She was finally alone.

Poppy hated every second of it.

Chapter 2

POPPY'S EYES felt dry and itchy. She didn't know how long she had cried, but surely, it must have been hours. The sky had grown dark since she had been jilted, and even though it was dinnertime, she was not hungry. She doubted she would ever eat again.

She flinched when she heard a knock on the door then her oldest brother's low, deep voice. "Pop, it's Chris. May I come in?"

"It doesn't matter anymore." Everyone had already seen her in her most humiliating moment.

The door opened and Christopher stepped in. He had changed, thankfully, from his wedding clothes to his regular clothes that he wore when he was working at the ranch. He looked at her softly which made her feel like she was five years old again.

Of all her brothers, Christopher had always been the most patient with her because he knew Poppy had been forced to grow up quickly after Mother's death.

"You should get out of these clothes and into your

nightgown." Christopher sat next to her and patted the top of her head. "I could ask Lucy to help unlace you."

"No, thank you."

"Are you hungry?"

"No."

There was an awkward silence before Christopher pulled her into a hug. "Everything will work itself out, Pop. We are going to be here for you. Just tell us what you need."

"Can you prevent me from being called an old maid? Being seen as a laughingstock?" Poppy asked coldly.

He winced as he kissed her forehead and started rubbing her back. "Oh, Poppy, I am so sorry. Richard is a coward and a cruel man for doing this to you. I swear to you, I will make him pay if he ever shows his face in Larkspur Valley again." He stared at her seriously. "If anyone makes ignorant remarks, let me know. I will make them regret ever treating you rudely."

She smiled. "Thank you. You are a good big brother."

Christopher stayed with her for a few minutes, telling her kindly about what a good sister she was before she dismissed him, telling him she was tired. As sympathetic as Chris was, he was still a man. A man could never understand a woman properly, let alone what she went through all her life.

A man could remain a bachelor all his life and it wouldn't affect him negatively in any way.

But being a spinster was a terrible fate. A rather lonely life. Poppy felt like an outcast in society. Not one of the married women but not a young schoolgirl, either. She didn't have a proper education nor did she have any talents to secure a proper job to earn her own money. Who would hire her anyway when she didn't know how to do anything?

Men would never understand how difficult a woman's life could be. Poppy sometimes felt like she had no control over her own fate. She had to wait for others to make the decisions for her.

Once she was alone again, Poppy lay back in the bed, staring at the ceiling. She had fallen in love three times, and all three men had broken her heart and abandoned her, either in the courting stage or on the day of her wedding. She had been a fool too many times.

She would not be a fool again and give her heart away.

But Poppy didn't want to stay in Larkspur Valley, either, where she would always be the poor, unlovable spinster. She also didn't want to be a burden to her siblings who all had growing families and didn't need to worry about her.

What Poppy needed to do was leave. A fresh start would do her good.

Her brothers would never let her leave on her own, though, especially Hugh and Christopher. Poppy closed her eyes, glad that forming an escape plan distracted her from her broken heart.

Finn was drunk. Or as close to drunk as he could ever be. He had never liked the taste of alcohol much, even if he was surrounded by men who drank the majority of the time. The whisky burned his throat as he glanced at the clock.

The Benningtons had finished their wedding feast by now. That jackass was taking Poppy to his bed right now, tearing her dress from her sweet little body, and maybe being rough with her despite her being an innocent virgin. He was supposed to be the only man in Poppy's life.

He had loved her for thirteen years, after all, and he was sure she felt something for him even if the stubborn little brat would never admit it.

It had taken all of Finn's willpower not to barge into the

church and steal the bride away. Steve had warned him not to even try or he would easily have him arrested, not to mention Poppy would have killed him if he ruined her wedding.

Despite the fact that Poppy had not chosen him, he still wanted her to be happy. If she was happy with Richard, there was nothing Finn could do but accept it and move on.

The door burst open and Finn flinched, his hand reaching to his gun which was strapped to his side. He never took it off except when he was bathing or in bed, and even then, he always had some type of weapon close.

Hugh Bennington stood in the center of the room like an angry wolf puffing and growling. It amazed him how Christopher, Steve, and Anthony were so calm, but Hugh and Poppy always seemed to have a short fuse.

"Why are you barging in like a lunatic?"

It didn't take much to make Hugh angry, but he looked absolutely furious right now. Did it have something to do with his twin? If it did, Finn would follow whatever foolish plan he had cooked up.

"He stood her up," Hugh growled. "Left her at the altar. My sister who's been wanting to get married for years. Humiliated her in front of half the town. When I find him, he'll be lucky if I leave him with any teeth."

Finn blinked, stunned. "Richard?"

"Who else, you fool?"

Finn felt his shoulders relax as relief spread through his body. Poppy wasn't a married woman after all. He had never heard such wonderful news. "How is she?"

"Devastated. Humiliated. She hasn't stopped crying."

Finn wanted nothing more than to pull Poppy into his arms and comfort her until she forgot all about Richard. Finn had always hated seeing her cry, even when she was being a moody brat or on the rare occasions when he had spanked her when she broke a rule or was misbehaving.

"Get your gun and your horse and follow me."

"Why?"

"Because you and I are going to search every nook and cranny until we find that selfish bastard and make him pay for hurting my sister. No one hurts Poppy, especially after everything she's been through."

Before Finn could respond, Christopher and Steve stormed in looking exhausted. Steve glared at his younger brother. "Stop acting like a headless chicken, Hugh. Richard is long gone. You'll never find him and it doesn't matter if he has fled. Our priority right now is Poppy."

"Our sister got her heart broken. Again. You might be willing to step aside, Steve, but I will not."

While Steve and Hugh bickered, Finn approached Christopher, who looked like he wanted to smack both of his brothers. "How is she doing?"

"She's a twenty-seven-year-old spinster whose groom ran off on their wedding day." Christopher had a worried expression on his face. "But she's Poppy. She'll survive and we'll be with her every step of the way."

"I will as well," Finn insisted firmly. "I've been a part of her life for thirteen years. I won't stop now."

Chapter 3

FINN MADE sure his light hair was slicked back before he grabbed the bouquet of flowers he had managed to pick that morning. It was quite a pitiful display, but there weren't many options in the middle of winter. He would just have to promise to pick something prettier once spring came.

He wasn't dressed in his Sunday best because he didn't want to make Poppy uncomfortable, and instead, he had just picked clean work clothes which didn't have any rips or permanent stains.

It had been a few days since Poppy had been left at the altar and the town was still talking about the jilted bride. Christopher had mentioned Poppy had finally left her bedroom, but she was still sad, which was understandable. He would never understand why Richard had left such a spitfire like Poppy, but he was glad he had.

Finn didn't want anyone else to have her.

He knew her wounds were still fresh, but he hoped in time, she would heal and would allow him to court her properly. Finn would marry Poppy a dozen times if she asked.

When he arrived at the Benningtons' second home where the unmarried ladies stayed, Finn frowned. Something was wrong.

He quickly recognized Christopher, Steve, Hugh, and Anthony's horses. All four men should be at work, and while the Benningtons had been taking extra care of Poppy, there was no reason why all four of them should be there on a weekday. Usually, they would just drop off their wives, Ruby or Lucy, to keep Poppy company while the younger girls were at school.

Finn felt a pit in his stomach. He hoped Poppy hadn't committed some kind of stupidity.

The blonde could sometimes act without thinking which, in the past, had earned her a light spanking or two from him over her skirts.

He stepped inside, not bothering to knock. The scene inside was a mess. Iris and Lily looked like they had been crying. Hugh was muttering angrily to himself while he crumpled a piece of paper in his hand. Lucy was rubbing Christopher's back, her pregnant belly against his body. Ruby was clutching Steve's arm while he carried Silver. Anthony stood grimacing across from him.

The bouquet suddenly felt heavy in his hand. "What's wrong?"

"This." Hugh shoved the paper in his hand.

Finn quickly scanned it, his frown growing. This couldn't be real. Poppy was gone. The letter didn't say much, only that she loved her family, she was sorry to do this, and that she needed a fresh start because she didn't want to become a burden to her family. Of course, she had conveniently left out where she was planning on going.

"That little fool!" Finn snarled as he crumpled the letter in his hand. He turned back to the brothers. "She could get hurt, or worse. The deserted countryside is no place for a woman. What on earth was she thinking?"

"Don't you think we know that?" Hugh snarled, looking like he wanted to punch Finn in the face. "I didn't tell my twin to run away."

"She's been gone for hours," Anthony continued quietly. "The ticket conductor at the station told us she boarded a six o'clock morning train headed to Laramie. Iris didn't notice she was gone until eleven in the morning because she thought she wanted to be alone. She could be in Laramie or she could be long gone, taking a carriage somewhere or getting off before she arrived in Laramie."

"We can still catch her," Hugh insisted, sounding like a mad man. "She's just one woman who has never left Larkspur Valley, with very little money in her pockets. How far could she have gotten?"

"Pop is more intelligent than we've ever given her credit for, apparently," Steve clipped as he kissed the top of Silver's head. "She managed to plan this in a matter of days."

Christopher jerked from Lucy's embrace; obviously the comment stung. "I won't ever forgive myself if Poppy gets hurt. We're her brothers, we are supposed to save her from danger, even from herself. Let's divide ourselves up and search for her. Finn, if you could stay with the girls—"

"No." Finn's jaw clenched. "I'm sorry, Chris, but I am not standing here doing nothing while Poppy is wandering around God knows where. If you are looking for her, I will as well."

"I'll stay behind," Anthony offered. "Finn is a faster rider than I am."

"Fine." Christopher kissed Lucy quickly. "Let's go find our sister."

The Bennington brothers, plus Finn, didn't find her that

day or the next. Before Finn knew it, two weeks had passed with no sign of her. They had divided themselves up and searched Laramie and the neighboring towns, but it was like Poppy had disappeared into thin air. No one had seen the blonde and it was driving Finn and the Benningtons mad with worry.

"You don't have to do this, Finn," Christopher insisted as he watched Finn pack a bag with clean clothes. "Poppy is our sister; she is our responsibility. You shouldn't have to be galloping all over Wyoming trying to find her. I think both of us are a little exhausted. We should wait. Eventually, Poppy's money will run out. She has never worked a day in her life, so she'll write or return home."

"I can't wait." Finn closed his bag. "I haven't slept a wink since Poppy left and I won't until I know she's safe and under someone's watchful eye. Someone has to keep searching for her and you and your brothers have your responsibilities. You have the ranch, and your wife is in the family way, Steve is the sheriff with a wife and daughter at home, Hugh is the only doctor in Larkspur Valley, and Anthony runs the church. I'm a single man. I do not have any responsibilities."

Christopher looked away guiltily as he stuffed Finn's hands with a large amount of bills. "Take it, use it for food, housing, and payment. Come back any time, even if you don't find her. We'll understand. We never thought Poppy would do this to us. We don't deserve your kindness or your loyalty."

"You have done enough. You gave me a job when I was a poor boy from Virginia without a penny to his name and ripped boots. I am just repaying your kindness. You have been a good boss, Christopher. Rest assured, whether it takes me a week or a year, I will bring your sister back."

Then I will marry her and make her my wife.

Chapter 4

FIVE MONTHS LATER, *July 1872...*

"Meet Lloyd Bennington." Christopher beamed proudly at his newborn son who was barely three weeks old as he placed the tiny bundle in Finn's arms. Finn had been meaning to visit sooner when he had received word from Hugh that Lucy had delivered her baby, but there simply hadn't been time.

It seemed for the past five months, he had hardly slept or eaten. Instead, he was constantly on horseback searching for the elusive Poppy Bennington. When Finn finally got his hand on her, and he would, he was going to whip her bottom good, until the idea of sitting only became a pleasant memory.

During the last five months, there hadn't even been a glimpse of Poppy despite the fact Steve had sheriffs from other neighboring towns keeping an eye out for her. Hugh kept ads in newspapers going in all of Wyoming. Christopher was offering a hefty reward for any clue that would lead to the retrieval of his wayward sister.

Finn smiled at he stared at the sleeping bundle of joy in

front of him who gave a tiny yawn. He had chubby cheeks and Lucy's own curly brown hair, something which overjoyed the proud papa.

"He's adorable. How is Lucy?"

"Resting. He might look innocent, but he's a menace. Lloyd keeps us up with his crying all night, so Lucy is a little sleep deprived. Hugh says he should sleep through the night in a few months. Ruby helped us out for the first few weeks, but now that Silver is crawling, she's harder to keep still. She broke two of Lucy's teacups the last time she was here."

Finn forced a smile as he returned Lloyd back into Chris' waiting arms. He was happy for both Christopher and Lucy, but he would be lying if he said he wasn't feeling a bit fidgety. Seeing Lloyd and Silver only reminded him that time was flying by and he was still no closer to finding Poppy. He didn't want the kids to grow up without an aunt and he knew Poppy would hate herself in the future for spending so much time away from her family.

Christopher seemed to read his mind because he looked at him kindly. "You can rest, Finn. Take a few months off; it will be good for you. We have been searching for Pop for five months and we are still no closer to finding her. You must have searched half of Wyoming by now. We are eternally grateful for your determination, but perhaps we should let Poppy decide when she is ready to come home."

"No." Finn threw him a dirty look. "If we stop now, we will never find her. We might never see her again, and I don't like the idea of a lonely, heartbroken woman traveling alone."

Christopher sighed. "I know, but Poppy is twenty-seven-years-old. She's a grown woman, Finn, despite her childish antics. If she hasn't come home by now, perhaps she is adjusting well. She has a good head on her shoulders. Maybe she needed space, to think clearly." He raised an eyebrow.

"Don't be a martyr, Finn. You can't spend your entire life searching for someone who doesn't want to be found."

Finn scowled at him. "I'm heading out. Congratulations on the baby. Please give Lucy my best."

Christopher sighed. "Where are you headed now?"

"Carson."

Carson was a small town, a seven days' journey south from Larkspur Valley. It was a stretch that Poppy would be there. From what Steve had told him, the town's population was very small. People only stopped by to get a bite to eat or find a bed for the night.

But this was the last town on his list before he started heading north or east. Perhaps Chris was right and he was being a fool. For all he knew, Poppy had scraped together enough money and was on a ship to Europe by now.

Finn's eyelids felt heavy from lack of sleep. Even when he stopped at night, he didn't fully sleep, for fear of robbers, and now he was paying the price. His muscles ached from being on horseback for days on end and his clothes and face were covered with dust.

He made a mental note to get some food at whichever restaurant was open and to rent a room at the nearest hotel for the night even if it was an absurd extravagance.

Please be here, Pop, he prayed silently as he arrived in Carson. *I would follow you to the ends of the earth, but I don't think my body would handle it.*

"Excuse me, where can I find a decent hotel with food service around here?" he asked gruffly to a pair of older looking men wearing dirty clothes, obviously on their lunch break.

The older of the two pointed his cigar towards a sad looking two-story yellow building which looked worse for wear. "The Pear Tree Hotel has cheap beds and a cook who can make a decent pot roast. View's nice too."

The other man snickered and Finn ignored the innuendos as he nodded his thanks. Once he made sure his horse had some water to drink, he made his way inside the small café attached to the hotel. It was filled with a lively bunch enjoying their lunch before they had to head back.

A tall, busty redhead with her hair in braids and a missing front tooth motioned him to follow her impatiently before she led him to a small table near the back. She pointed to the pitiful looking menu written in chalk.

"Your girl will be with you soon."

Before Finn could respond, she was already making her way to the kitchen. Finn sighed as he looked at the menu. There wasn't any pot roast, but there was roast beef with mashed potatoes and pea soup.

"Sorry to keep you waiting, sir. May I take your order?"

Finn's head jerk back so fast, he was surprised his neck hadn't broken in half. *That voice.* He knew that voice. It had been haunting him in his dreams ever since she had disappeared after her almost disastrous wedding.

Standing in front of him, was the jilted bride.

Poppy Bennington.

Except, this Poppy was different from the one he had known since his adolescence. The Poppy he knew was always well-groomed, wearing decent clothes, and always, without fail, had a haughty, arrogant expression on her lovely face. The woman standing in front of him might as well be a complete stranger because he did not recognize her.

Her blonde hair was tangled and pulled back in a low bun. The brown dress she was wearing was ugly and dirty from food and seemed to hang from her scrawny body. Her cheeks were sunken from a lack of proper food and the last time she had looked so exhausted was when Lily had been a baby.

Poppy was used to hard work, but working as a substitute

mother for Iris and Lily was different than working as a waitress for little pay and no additional income. Poppy had always had money readily available, given to her by her father or brothers, and plenty to eat. Life outside the Bennington ranch had proven to be difficult.

The remaining color which had been on her face drained completely. "Finn."

Finn stood up, nearly knocking the chair over. He gripped her slender shoulders as if he was afraid she would disappear. "Found you."

Chapter 5

FOR A SECOND, Poppy didn't move. She kept staring at him as if she wasn't sure if he was real or not. Then she started to squirm like a fish out of water trying to get out of Finn's grip, but it was nearly impossible because he was holding her too tightly.

She had escaped once; he wasn't going to allow her to do it again. Finn would tie her to him if it came to it.

Finn noticed the customers of the café, who were mainly men, were staring at them with amusement, their eyes focusing on Poppy. Anger settled in the pit of Finn's stomach. He didn't consider himself a violent man, but at that moment, he wanted nothing more than to punch every man who was staring at Poppy in a less than respectful way.

"Let me go!" Poppy said under her breath, her blue eyes narrowing at him angrily.

"And let you escape again? Never," Finn hissed back.

She was obviously embarrassed by this spectacle, but he didn't care. Poppy pulled back, which only caused Finn to tighten his grip around her wrist instead of her shoulders, causing her to yelp.

Poppy's lower lip trembled. "Finn, you're hurting me."

Finn knew she was exaggerating—it wasn't like he was bruising her—but he loosened his grip slightly. "Then come with me and we can talk like adults without providing a spectacle," he suggested calmly.

Poppy closed her eyes as if she couldn't bear to look at him. "No."

Finn raised his eyebrow in a mocking way. "I tried to ask nicely, Pop. Please remember that." Before she could inquire what he meant by that, he placed both hands on her waist, raised her up, and draped her over his shoulder.

The blonde squealed in protest, like one of the baby piglets he had raised back on his farm in Virginia, as he felt her stomach dig into his shoulder. Poppy started slapping his back angrily and Finn responded by landing a loud smack on her rump which quieted her down immediately.

The men from the café started to cheer which irritated Finn, while the redheaded woman who had greeted him at the beginning stood by the kitchen door with her mouth open in shock.

A dark-haired man approached Finn with a determined look on his face. "If the lady does not want to go with you—"

Finn didn't let him finish before he landed a punch across his jaw, causing the man to fall to the floor. Maybe the Benningtons were starting to rub off on him after years of working for them.

"You hit him!" Poppy stared at him in shock. "You never hit anyone. You're not like Hugh. Why did you do that?"

"Because he was in my way. Now, Poppy, be quiet."

Thankfully, Poppy did as she was told. Neither of them talked until they reached his horse.

"If I let you go, will you promise to behave?" Poppy nodded as Finn slowly let her down. "If you try to run away, I will spank you in the middle of the town square."

Poppy blushed as she slowly nodded. She was no stranger to Finn spanking her; it had been the main reason why she had rejected his proposals so many times. It was always over her skirts, though, to preserve her modesty. Though, one time when she had risked her life along with Lucy, he had spanked her on the bare rump. It was clear she did not want to repeat that given how mad he looked.

"How did you find me?"

"There's no place you can hide from me, Poppy."

Poppy snorted.

"Where are you staying?" Finn asked gruffly as he untied the horse. Poppy didn't say anything and, instead, just looked at her tattered shoes. It was unlike her to be so quiet; usually, her sharp tongue got her in trouble often. Finn gripped her wrist. "Dammit, Poppy. You have already earned yourself a hard spanking. Don't add to your list of offenses."

Poppy widened her blue eyes. "Why are you being so mean? You've never been this mean before."

Finn raised an eyebrow. "You mean, you could manipulate me easier before."

Poppy blushed but didn't argue.

Finn forced himself to calm down. Poppy had been through a lot and by the look on her face and her clothes, it hadn't been an easy five months for her, either. He had to get her home to her brothers without killing her first.

"Poppy, tell me where are you staying. Otherwise, we can go from door to door asking all of the neighbors."

"The boarding house," Poppy finally whispered after a while.

He nodded and gently helped Poppy on top of the horse while she gave him directions. The small boarding house was only a few feet away from the hotel and was run by a mean old woman who introduced herself as Mrs. Griff and looked like she hadn't smiled a day in her life.

"No men upstairs, Miss Collins," Mrs. Griff barked. "This boardinghouse is for women only. I run a respectable establishment."

Finn pulled out some money and handed it to her. "I can assure you, you can look the other way just this once, ma'am." Mrs. Griff snorted before she greedily took the money.

"Miss Collins?" Finn asked as Poppy led him to a small, upstairs bedroom.

"I changed my last name. I didn't want my brothers finding me," she responded dryly as she opened the door. "I guess I shouldn't have bothered."

"I will always find you, Pop."

Poppy threw him a dirty look. He simply smiled. At least she was getting her spark back.

The bedroom Poppy was renting at the boarding house was barely larger than an outhouse. There was a small bed, a little wardrobe which would barely fit three dresses, and a tiny table with a broken pitcher and bowl to wash her face in.

She seemed embarrassed by her little bedroom and he couldn't believe she had actually lived there for months. A girl like Poppy deserved a warm bed and to be safe from the shady characters he had seen roaming around the town.

"How did you find me?" she finally asked. "I want the truth this time."

"I've been traveling to a new town or city for months. Your brothers helped me at the beginning, but they have their own jobs and responsibilities, so it has been mainly I who has been searching for you." He took a step forward until his muscled chest was touching her back. He placed a hand on her shoulder, expecting her to pull away, but she didn't. "Why did you run, Poppy?"

"I couldn't bear the humiliation. Courted by three

different men in almost ten years and yet none of them wanted to commit to me. One even ran away screaming on our wedding day because he couldn't bear to be married to me." She smiled bitterly. "I refuse to be a laughingstock in that town, Finn. They already called me the bitter, sharp-tongued old maid. I refused to be labeled a cautionary tale, or worse, be the object of their pity."

"But what about your family? They've been worried sick over you. Don't you miss them?" he demanded. "Silver started to walk and Lucy gave birth to a baby boy named Lloyd. Do you really want your niece and nephew to grow up without an aunt?"

Poppy flinched. "I can always visit. It's only a few days' trip away from Larkspur Valley."

"Dammit, Poppy, you don't belong here living in this pigsty and working yourself half to death. You should be married and focused on taking care of your own home."

"That's the point, Finn," she scowled, turning around to stare at him as if he were an idiot. "*No one wants to marry me. The only way you're going to take me back to Larkspur Valley is if you bring me in a coffin.*"

"Poppy," he warned. "You have one minute to start packing your bags or I will paddle your little behind and then take you to Larkspur Valley; it's entirely your choice."

She narrowed her eyes angrily at him. "Make me."

Finn's eyes focused on the hairbrush sitting innocently against the broken pitcher and immediately grabbed it. He then bent Poppy against the table, his hand wrapped tightly around her waist so she couldn't escape his grasp.

"You can't spank me, stop it!" she hissed as he pushed up her skirts and hastily pulled down her petticoats and drawers, leaving her small, pale behind bare. "You're not my husband."

"Honey, if I were your husband, I would have given you a good thrashing a long time ago to tame your pride and arrogance. You're too hardheaded; you need a good spanking sometimes to make you think things through thoroughly. If it were up to me, you would have married and had a few babies to settle you down years ago, but your brothers didn't want to order you around and that was their mistake."

"Go to hell!" she screamed, the tears springing in her eyes as she thrashed around like an angry kitten.

Finn chuckled, glad to have the little spitfire back instead of the wallflower from earlier. "Well, your bottom is going to be as hot as hell soon."

Through her squirming, he could see the golden curls of her mound and her sweet, tight little slit. He wanted nothing more than to part her legs and make her his woman, but he would have to wait until he finished disciplining her.

Her bottom was small, heart-shaped, pale. This wasn't the first time he had spanked her. He had spanked her before, for being a rude little thing, but it had always been a light spanking. Of course, Poppy had screamed bloody murder even back then. She didn't know how hard he could slap her little bottom.

Finn gripped her hairbrush in his hand before landing it firmly against her right cheek, leaving behind a pink, oval print. Poppy screamed. Finn ignored her.

Instead, he only concentrated on landing a smack on the other cheek. The room filled with the sounds of *thwack, thwack, thwack* as the heavy hairbrush landed on her tender nates, turning them from pink to red.

"Stop it! Stop it!" she cried out as tears poured down her face.

Finn ignored her request as he watched her bottom cheeks bounce against the hairbrush. The round cheeks were bright red and hot to the touch. Poppy would have a hard time sitting on the saddle for days to come. Good.

"You were very naughty, Poppy, running away from home." He slapped down the brush across the back of each thigh, causing them to bloom pink as well. Poppy unwillingly spread her legs, giving him a lovely view of her womanhood which was covered with her dewiness.

He shifted uncomfortably, trying to ignore the fact that his trousers had become unbearably tight.

"You could have gotten killed or hurt."

Smack.

"Your siblings and their wives were worried sick."

Smack.

"You will never do such a silly thing like that again. Understood?"

He rubbed her sore butt, his hand cupping the swollen cheeks while she rubbed her ass against his hand, wanting him to rub the soreness away.

Poppy didn't respond to his scolding, but she did dig her little nails against the table as he finished administering some much-needed punishment.

Finn placed down the hairbrush on the small table before helping her up and dressing her again. He smoothed down her petticoats and then her thin dress before forcing her to face him, even though she was jumping around like a cat who had been sprayed with water.

"Get your things *now.*"

She opened her mouth, probably to tell him something rude.

"Do you want another spanking?"

Poppy reluctantly shook her head as she started packing the little bag she had taken with her. Ten minutes later, they were out the door, leaving a shocked Mrs. Griff, who had probably overheard the whole thing, behind. He placed her on the horse, ignoring the groan as her sore cheeks touched the saddle.

"Hang on to me," he ordered gruffly. When she refused to do so, he let out a small curse under his breath, grabbed both of her arms from behind and forced her to wrap them around his torso. Her large breasts rubbed against his back, and he could feel the hard little pebbles which awoke his manhood. "Your day would go much better if you just did as you were told."

They rode in silence for a few more minutes until they stood in front of a tiny church.

"What are we doing here? Praying for my soul?"

Finn ignored her sarcastic response as he helped her down. "No. We are going to get married."

A panicked look settled on Poppy's face as she looked down at the dirty dress. "Are you insane? We can't get married, especially when I'm dressed like this."

"You told me you wouldn't return to Larkspur Valley as a spinster, so I am giving you the option to return as a married woman."

"You haven't even proposed."

"I have proposed to you several times. You just haven't accepted them. I'm not giving you the choice now."

"All right, but we should really return to Larkspur Valley first. I should be properly married by my brother in the church I grew up in."

"And give you a chance to escape again or to go crying to your brothers about what a brute I am? No, thank you. We're not leaving until you are Mrs. Finn Weston." *And preferably with my baby in your belly.* "Perhaps that will make you think twice about running away from your problems."

"You don't have a ring," she announced flatly.

Finn smirked as he pulled out a small green velvet box and showed her the dainty gold ring with pearls and diamonds. The same ring he had proposed to her with for years. It had cost him a small fortune at the time, but Poppy was worth it.

Poppy bit her lower lip. "You've been carrying it with you?"

"Always." He offered his hand and she took it instead of slapping it away. "Now, let's get married, Pop."

Chapter 6

POPPY HAD BEEN Mrs. Weston for exactly seven days when they finally arrived back in Larkspur Valley. Though, in her heart, she would always remain Miss Bennington.

The town looked exactly the same as it always had. She didn't know why she had expected it to look different. She had been gone for only five months after all. Or maybe she was different.

Her muscles ached from riding a horse for days, and she suddenly didn't want to do anything but crawl into her childhood bed and sleep for hours. She and Finn had either stayed in small inns or camped during their journey, which didn't help her crankiness.

Both she and Finn had been in sour moods since they left town, arguing over every little thing.

However, the ring glistening in the sun reminded her she was very much married. She doubted Finn would let her go easily. She was just glad they could head to the Benningtons' second home without crossing through town. Poppy wasn't ready to deal with the humiliation yet. How would she explain running away and then coming back married?

It would be hard enough to explain to her family why she married Finn. Or why Finn forced her to marry him.

Finn placed a hand on her shoulder as they overlooked the town. "Are you all right?"

Poppy was grateful Finn had been behaving like a gentleman throughout their trip, because if he tried to kiss her or consummate their marriage, she would have gladly bitten him.

She nodded shrewdly. "Yes. Let's just go."

When they stood in front of the second Bennington home that she and her sisters had moved into after Chris married Lucy, she felt her heart stop inside her chest. Poppy felt a mixture of emotions—sadness, happiness, and perhaps a little embarrassment thrown in because she had returned with her tail between her legs.

Finn had told her he had sent a telegram informing them of their return, though he wasn't sure if it had arrived on time.

Finn raised an eyebrow. "Do you need me to carry you?"

Poppy scowled as she stopped at the door.

Finn pressed a hand gently against her lower back. "What's wrong, Pop?" he murmured in her ear, his lips barely brushing against it, causing a shiver to go down her spine.

"I'm scared," she finally admitted, allowing herself to be vulnerable in front of Finn. "I've been gone for six months. I've missed the birth of Lloyd and watching Silver grow up. They must have been out of their minds with worry. What if they hate me for running away, for worrying them? What if they never forgive me?"

"They will, sugar." Finn pressed his thumb and index finger against her chin to force her to look at him. "You are their sister, practically their second mother. They knew you were going through a lot with Richard. They will understand why you did what you did. You shouldn't have run away, but the important thing is I found you. Besides, I already took care of your punishment. All you have to worry about now is moving on and spending a lot of time spoiling your niece and nephew."

Poppy scowled at him when he mentioned her punishment. She hadn't been sitting comfortably the entire journey. A fact she reminded him of often.

Finn used the opportunity to push the door open, giving both of them a glimpse of the entire family. Lily and Iris were on the floor playing with Silver, Anthony and Hugh had been conversing in the back while Steve and Ruby cooed over a tiny bundle she guessed was baby Lloyd. Meanwhile, Lucy was curled up in Christopher's arms while he nervously tugged on her brown curls.

Poppy felt like someone was sitting on her chest, making it hard to breathe. She continued blinking her blue eyes as if she couldn't believe the sight in front of her. It had been six months since she had seen her family. She couldn't believe how much she had missed them. The past few months had been terribly lonely.

Lily was the first to react. She immediately got up and raced into her arms, nearly tossing her down. Lily had gotten so tall and was blossoming into a pretty young woman. Pretty soon, she would be putting up her hair and letting down her skirts. But for now, she was still little Lily, practically a baby still.

"You're back." Lily smelled of the sweet violets and larkspur flowers which surrounded the Bennington ranch. "Oh, Pop, why did you leave?"

Poppy's throat felt tight and she was afraid she would cry. "I'm sorry."

"We missed you," Iris continued, wrapping her own arms around Poppy's lanky shoulders. Iris' face was blotchy and red like it often was when she was feeling overwhelmed with feelings.

Silver clapped, obviously happy that everyone else was thrilled.

"I missed all of you too." The tears were threatening to spill, but she refused to allow it. She hated crying in front of people. "I'm glad to be home again."

Her twin pulled Lily and Iris off her so he could embrace her himself. Hugh's hug was bone crushing and she was surprised by the gesture. The last time he had hugged her had been at their father's funeral.

"Don't ever commit such a stupidity again, Poppy," he growled in her ear. "Do you understand me? Richard was not worth this ordeal you put us through. He's lucky he skipped town; otherwise, all of his pretty teeth would be missing."

"I'm sorry, Hugh." She hadn't realized how hard it had been to be away from her twin. They had been attached to each other's hip since birth, and even when Hugh was away at medical school, he still managed to write weekly letters to her.

"Oh, Poppy, you little devil, where did you run off too?" Ruby grinned at her. "While I'm glad you are all right, I hope you have some interesting stories to tell us."

Steve pinched his wife's cheek. "Don't encourage her, Ruby." He kissed his sister's forehead. "Welcome back, Pop. I don't know how Finn managed to drag you back, but I'm grateful. I hadn't realized how much I missed your tantrums."

Ruby whacked him on the shoulder while she rolled her eyes. Silver crawled towards her and showed her a toothless grin. She picked her up and kissed her forehead then let her down on the floor. "There's my beautiful girl."

Poppy smiled as Anthony wrapped an arm around her

shoulders. It felt great being surrounded by family again. Why had she ever thought about leaving in the first place?

Christopher placed a hand on Poppy's shoulder before he pulled her into a tight, bone crushing hug, causing Silver to squeal as she lay on the floor between them.

"You're crushing her, Chris," she scolded him, but Chris ignored her as Ruby discreetly grabbed her daughter back.

"Never ever do that again, Poppy Bennington. I mean it. You had us worried sick," he scolded furiously as he patted the back of her head in a loving but stern way.

"We're glad you're back," his wife, Lucy, said in a much more loving manner as she presented her with the small bundle. "There is someone I want you to meet. This is Lloyd. Lloyd, this is Aunt Poppy."

Lloyd gurgled something at her before he went back to sleep. Poppy sniffed as she touched his head. "Oh, Lucy, he's beautiful. Congratulations to both of you." She looked around. "And thank you all for such a warm welcome."

Lily cocked her small face to the side. "Where have you been all this time, Poppy?"

Before she could answer, her twin grasped her wrist and raised it so everyone could see. His blue eyes flashed dangerously. "Is this a wedding ring? Who are you married to?"

Her siblings stared back at her in shock. Poppy felt herself turn bright red.

"Did Richard come back?" Iris squealed.

"He'd better not!" Hugh growled.

"Poppy?" Steve folded his arms across his chest. "Explain please, before we need to restrain Hugh."

Poppy looked timidly at Finn for support.

"Poppy and I got married," Finn announced firmly as he placed a gentle hand around her waist, causing her to feel protected. "She was in a small town about a seven days' journey from here. She's Mrs. Weston now. I promise I will take care of her and give her an honorable life."

For a second, there was nothing but stunned silence. Even Christopher looked shocked as if he couldn't believe his best friend and right-hand man had married his sister even though he had been pining for her for years.

"You son-of-a-bitch, did you force her? I'm going to kill you!" Hugh roared as he pounced towards Finn. Anthony and Steve, who were closer to him, had the good sense to pull him away while he continued to yell out curse words.

"Hugh, no one forced me!" Poppy protested as she placed a hand against his chest to prevent Finn from being killed by her twin. Though Finn didn't look the least bit concerned and was instead just staring at her brother politely. "I married him because I wanted to."

Hugh scowled at her. "Do you expect me to believe that? You've been rejecting him for years, and the minute he decides to play hero, you suddenly come back married?"

"I would never force a woman to do anything she didn't want to do, especially your sister," Finn argued coldly. Finn didn't strike Poppy as a violent man, but the past few days had proven to her that perhaps she didn't know Finn as well as she thought she did.

"No one is saying that." Anthony tried to keep the peace. "We are just a little surprised, that's all, given your past relationship with Pop."

"Are you in the family way?" Steve blurted out, looking at his little sister's stomach. Ruby slapped his shoulder while Hugh's eyes turned even more murderous than they already were.

"No!" Poppy looked offended. "Of course not. We only married to protect my reputation is all, since I've been gone for too long. People in town have surely been talking about my disappearance. A marriage makes things respectable at least."

"Who cares what they say? You didn't have to marry Finn." Hugh glared at Anthony. "They can have this ridiculous marriage annulled, can't they?"

"We will stay married. This marriage is very real, whether you choose to believe it or not. We were married in front of a pastor. I will take good care of your sister; you can count on it." Finn stood firmly, glancing at the rest of the Bennington men who had grown upset.

"Why don't you boys talk outside?" Lucy offered as she squeezed her husband's hand. "Poor Poppy must be starving, and we need to put the babies down for a nap."

Once the women managed to steer the men outside, Lucy turned back to Poppy with her hands on her hips. "Explain, Poppy. I believe you owe us an explanation after everything."

So, Poppy did. She told them her reasons for leaving, the terrible five months she spent working as a waitress at a nearby town, and finally, how Finn had found her and forced her to marry him to get some of her pride back, but mainly to keep an eye on her.

Lily let out a little sigh as she played with Silver who was drooling everywhere. "That is so romantic."

Poppy scowled. "How is marrying someone in an empty church and wearing dirty clothes romantic?"

"He didn't want you to feel ashamed when you came back to town. He wanted you to be able to return with your head held high," Iris said gently. "His heart was in the right place."

"For someone who doesn't want to get married ever, I thought you would be on my side," Poppy murmured.

Iris shrugged. "I am on the side of logic."

Ruby nodded as she picked up Silver and placed her on

her breast. "She's right; if Finn wouldn't have married you, then you would have every door closed in your face. Believe me, it is horrid being on the opposite end where everyone treats you like a toad."

Ruby had been a prostitute before Steve married her and got her pregnant with Silver.

"I didn't want to come back," Poppy whispered childishly.

Lucy looked hurt. "Didn't you miss us?"

"Of course, I did. I'm sorry, that was such a horrid thing to say." Poppy bit into one of the cookies Lucy had baked. "I am just not looking forward to having people talking about me for the next few months."

"They'll talk about how handsome your husband is and how you're the lucky devil who snagged him." Ruby's eyes twinkled with mischief. She'd never liked the town women. "For Finn, there has been no one else but you, Poppy."

"Perhaps this is God's way of telling you to give him a chance," Lucy reprimanded gently. "He's a good man and he loves you so. I know he will make a good husband."

Poppy nodded as she looked at a sleeping Lloyd, suddenly longing for her own child. "I know."

Poppy was dying to tell Ruby and Lucy about her previous spanking, but she was too embarrassed to bring it up in front of her little sisters. She would have to talk to them in private later.

Lily hugged her tightly again. "I'm glad you're home again, Pop. The house was just not the same without you. Iris is too bossy. She'll be a mean teacher someday."

Iris reddened. "I am not. You're just too lazy."

Lily stuck out her tongue.

Iris rolled her eyes.

"Though I suppose this is no longer your house. You will

be moving to Finn's home after he and the men finish talking," Lucy mused.

Her sisters sobered.

Panic entered her chest. She hadn't thought about moving in with Finn. She had never lived with a man before, other than her brothers and father. She put on a brave smile for her sisters. "Don't worry. Finn's house… our house is only a few miles away. We will still see each other plenty."

"I won't apologize for marrying your sister." Finn glared at the Bennington brothers who were looking at him calmly, with the exception of Hugh, who looked ready to strangle him. "It was the right thing to do at the time, not to mention, your sister needs a husband to take care of her."

"We'll see if you still think it was the right thing to do once I crush your nose with my fist," Hugh growled.

Steve rolled his eyes. "Enough. What's done is done. They are married; there is nothing more that can be done."

Anthony cocked his head to the side. "Has the marriage been consummated?"

Hugh groaned. "I don't want to hear that about my sister."

"I've properly married her. I will give a good, decent life to her and any children which come out of this marriage. She will not suffer with me." He looked at the men whom he had worked alongside with for years to the point they had become almost brothers. Now they were looking at him as if they weren't sure whether he was a friend or foe. "Your sister needs a husband."

"She doesn't need anything from you," Hugh snapped. "I'll take care of Poppy for the rest of my life. She will never want for anything. Christopher, let's get this ridiculous marriage annulled."

"No, he's right," Christopher said slowly, looking at Finn wryly. "She needs a husband. Poppy should have gotten married a long time ago. She needs to stop acting so childishly and focus on her own family instead of being a busybody. We have known Finn for years, and I believe we can trust him when he says he will take good care of Poppy."

Finn nodded. "Thank you for trusting me."

Christopher nodded. "A word of warning, Finn, don't mistake our gratitude for finding Poppy as acceptance. You shouldn't have married her without getting the approval of one of us. If you cause her harm in any way, you will have us to deal with."

Finn offered his hand. "The last thing I would ever want to do is hurt Poppy. She is safe with me."

After they talked for a few minutes, they made their way back into the house where the girls were finishing lunch. Lucy and Ruby were nowhere to be seen. They were probably putting the babies to sleep.

Poppy raised her head, then blushed when she looked at him.

Iris shifted nervously from foot to foot. "Would you like some lunch, Finn?"

"No, thank you, Iris. Poppy and I must go. I would like to give her a tour of the house before it gets dark. We will see you at church on Sunday. Perhaps, if Pop is feeling up to it, we'll all have dinner at our house after church."

"What about my stuff?" Poppy demanded.

"You can go upstairs and pack a few clothes for the next few days and we'll come for it on Saturday."

"We can help pack it," Lily chirped, completely oblivious to the tension in the room. "We can bring it over on Sunday. Anthony or Hugh can help us take it over."

Finn smiled. "Thank you, Lily. Now say your goodbyes, Poppy."

Poppy reluctantly did as she was told, but the glare she was giving him let him know she was not pleased with him. After she had said her goodbyes to her siblings and had Iris help her pack a few of her belongings, Poppy reluctantly allowed him to help her sit on top of the horse again.

Finn sighed as he nodded his goodbyes to the Benningtons. He hoped Poppy would lose some of her prickliness in the coming weeks. It would be tiring to fight her every minute of every day.

It took them about fifteen minutes to reach his small, two-story house with the neighboring barn behind it, along with the chicken coop. It wasn't anything fancy, but it made him proud that he had built it with his own two hands. It wasn't as grand as the house Poppy had grown up in, but he hoped she would like it all the same and hoped someday she would think of it as their home.

"This is my home. Well, our home," he stated as he helped her down from the horse. "It's not very grand, but it's sturdy. It will keep us warm in the winter. It has three bedrooms currently, but I can always add to it if necessary once the children come."

Poppy looked stunned at the mention of children, especially since they hadn't become man and wife yet.

Finn pressed a hand against her lower back. "Let me give you a tour."

The house was plain but tidy. As a man, he didn't know much about decorating so it was terribly uninteresting. He also didn't spend much time at home to care about decorations. "You can go shopping in town once you've settled down or you can order things from back east from the catalogs I get in the mail."

As a bachelor, he hadn't had many expenses, especially

since Chris provided food for his workers, so he had managed to save a nice, tidy amount. Enough to spoil his wife if he chose to. He wanted Poppy to be happy and have the nice things she was used to.

Though, Christopher had mentioned Poppy had handled the family's finances for years and she was good at saving money, unlike Lily and Ruby, who seemed to believe money grew on trees.

"The three bedrooms are upstairs, though only the main one has a bed. I don't have many guests." He cleared his throat. "Even though the outhouse is outside, I have a little room for privacy where you can wash up."

Finn pushed the door open to what was going to be their bedroom so his new wife could view it. It had a four-poster bed with two settees, an armoire for his own clothes and a chest of drawers.

"I'll buy you your own armoire and vanity so you are able to place your dresses and hats inside." Finn was rambling; he knew that. He wanted to slap himself for being so foolish. It seemed he finally realized Poppy Bennington had become his wife after years of begging and would be coming to live with him.

"It's not necessary," Poppy said quietly. "The furniture my siblings will bring from my bedroom is perfectly intact. They can bring my furniture and my bed—"

"Why would they bring your bed?" Finn interrupted, even though it was rude.

Poppy appeared scandalized. "What do you mean, why? You cannot be thinking we will be sharing a room? It's not appropriate!"

"And why not?" He raised an eyebrow as he placed his hands around her waist, forcing her to look at him. "We're married. A husband and wife share a bed, Poppy. It is the way God intended."

Poppy's face was bright red. "It's not a real marriage! You just married me so I didn't become the town laughingstock!"

"It is still a legal marriage, whether you deny it or not. The fact that we haven't consummated it can easily be remedied." Poppy paled. Finn placed a reassuring hand on the back of her head. "Don't worry. I will not pleasure you until you are ready, but, honey, eventually we will share a bed." He winked at her. "The only reason we'll sleep in different beds is if one of us is ill or if you're giving birth to our children."

Poppy didn't respond, but it was quite clear she was furious.

"Moving on, we have some less pleasant things to deal with. Mainly, your punishment." Finn clicked his tongue, his hand resting dangerously close to his belt buckle. "You did a very foolish thing, Poppy. You had your family and me worried sick for weeks. Your brothers spent a small fortune, not to mention time and resources, trying to find you, all because you couldn't communicate your feelings like the adult woman you claim to be. Well, now you are going to be punished exactly how you behaved, like a spoiled little girl." He unbuckled his belt.

Poppy's hands flew to her bottom, her eyes growing wide. "You already spanked me back at the boarding house! I already had my punishment."

"I paddled your rear end back at the boarding house because you were being a rude little thing who was refusing to come with me." He held the belt tightly in his hand. "This is for all the worry you caused me for months."

He could sense her moves before she even made them. She started running towards the door, her hand holding onto the doorknob.

Before she could turn it, he grabbed her by the waist, causing Poppy to start screaming hysterically. She attempted to get away from him, but he was much stronger. This wasn't the first time he had spanked her, so he wasn't sure why she was making such a ruckus.

The last time he had given her such a thorough spanking was when she and Lucy had put themselves in danger, almost two years ago.

Angry tears appeared in her eyes and while Finn would usually be sympathetic, currently, he just wanted to get the punishment over with so he and Poppy could move on with their marriage.

He supposed he could let it slide, but Finn realized he needed to put his foot down. Poppy had walked over him in the past. He didn't want to be a doormat in their marriage. Besides, she had run away and been gone for months. She deserved a sore rump for a day or two.

Poppy was his wife now, and she needed to understand she was no longer running the show. While, of course, her opinion would be taken into consideration in the future, Finn was to be the head of their household.

When Poppy was naughty, she would be spanked.

Finn sat down on their bed and draped an angry Poppy over his lap. In all honesty, it was like trying to control an angry cat. Even though she kicked, screamed, and tried to scratch him, he refused to let her go. Growing up on a farm with a large group of siblings, one angry little girl was the least of his worries.

"Take your punishment, Pop. It will be all over soon." Finn gritted his teeth when Poppy kicked her legs like an angry donkey.

"You can go to hell, Finn Weston!" she snarled.

Finn shook his head as he pulled up her skirts and bared her bottom over his lap. Poppy stopped squirming for a moment when she realized she was nude from the waist down.

Finn had seen her bare before, but his cock still stirred in his trousers whenever he saw her smooth, round cheeks. The female form was truly beautiful and he was convinced Poppy Weston was the epitome of female beauty. Perhaps it was because it had been a while since he had lain with a woman and he and Poppy hadn't had a proper wedding night.

He would give anything to find himself between her smooth thighs.

Shaking his head, he tightened the belt in his hand and rubbed it against the round, plump cheeks before he raised his arm again and brought it down, causing a loud *swish* to echo in the room.

His wife bucked over his lap, which caused his cock to jump in place, as well as earning him a glare from his wife which he ignored. He raised the belt again then brought it down firmly against both exposed cheeks. The pale flesh bloomed pink under the administration of the belt.

Poppy let out a shriek as she dug her nails against his thigh, which her husband promptly ignored as he continued whipping her with the belt.

Her once pale cheeks wobbled against the belt's swats, causing him to grow hard until he just wanted to undress and bury himself in his wife. Poppy's cheeks bounced erotically to the rhythm of his belt as he covered her ass with bright red strokes, making sure every inch of her porcelain skin was bright red.

When she parted her legs slightly, the belt caught her sensitive inner thighs and the pouty lips of her womanhood, causing her to moan out in pain. Finn inspected her red bottom which had grown swollen during her spanking and pinched a bit of the welted skin between his finger, making sure she had been appropriately punished.

At the thirtieth stroke, he stopped whipping her bottom and placed his belt back on the bed while she sobbed over his lap. His large hand stroked her red skin, feeling the welts and tender skin left behind which would leave her resting on her belly for days.

Poppy shivered over his lap as she buried her face in her hands while tears dripped down her face. He continued rubbing her bottom, wishing he had some ointment to sooth the pain, but they had arrived in town so suddenly, he hadn't had a chance to go to the general store.

"It's over, sweetheart. Your punishment is over," he cooed to her gently.

Once she was released from his grip, she practically jumped out of his lap and ran into the center of their bed as she clutched the pillows furiously against her chest. Her blue eyes glared at him angrily, a mixture of hatred, pain, and anger that caused the guilt to settle in his chest.

"I hate you," she hissed, "I hate you, Finn Weston! I hate you! I never wanted to marry you."

Her words hurt and they cut deeply into Finn. He wasn't sure if they were true or if she was angry because she had been spanked.

Still, it wouldn't do anyone any good to get upset. He had to be the bigger person even if her words hurt.

"I'm sorry you feel that way," he said calmly, "but we are married and we shall remain married until one of us is dead. I hope you remember that."

Poppy glared at him, tossing a pillow at his head which he easily dodged. "You are upset. Go to sleep. You're overtired. If you are feeling hungry later, come downstairs."

Without waiting for a response, he closed the door behind himself.

Chapter 7

POPPY'S EYES felt sore and dry by the time she cracked them open the following day. It was late. She could tell by the way the sun was pouring into her new bedroom. She forced herself up even though the only thing she wanted to do was hide under the covers to deal with this new, recent humiliation.

She had barely been Mrs. Weston for a little over a week and she and her husband were at odds. Not to mention, her butt was burning and sitting would only be a distant dream for the next few days.

Her fingers gently touched the welts which had been left behind by the belt. She closed her eyes, wincing when she felt the bumps on her fair skin which would itch while they healed. Her mind kept going back to the way her husband had punished her, swinging the belt over and over onto her defenseless rump. Even her cries hadn't stopped him.

Finn was a brute. An odious man. He might have been able to fool everyone with his sunny smile and pleasant demeanor, but he would never fool her.

It had been smart of him not to spend the night in their

bedroom because she would have surely decapitated him if he had.

A good wife would have been up to make her husband breakfast and kiss him goodbye on his way to work, but given that he had whipped her on what was supposed to be their wedding night, Finn deserved nothing more than cold toast.

The wedding night. She clutched the covers in her clammy hands. Finn and she might be at odd ends right now, but he was still her husband. Most of all, he was still a man, and she would be expected to submit to him at one point or another. Finn had already been more patient than most men.

Even though he had already seen her bare bottom and her quim by all the kicking she had done each time she was bent over, it was entirely different than being fully naked.

Mrs. Finn Weston had been a married woman for a week and she was still a fumbling virgin who would rather sweep the desert than allow a man to see her naked.

Ruby often joked she was a prude and that it had been the real reason why she had remained a spinster for so long. Poppy had ignored her teasing. She didn't know why women were expected to perform that incredibly embarrassing act over and over again just because men wanted it.

Outside of creating a family, what was the point of the matrimonial act? It was as intriguing to Poppy as a visit to the dentist.

Lucy said it was lovely with the right husband who was gentle. Poppy wasn't sure if she believed her.

Although she wanted children, Poppy was more than happy to wait a few more years if it meant she and Finn didn't have to see each other in the nude. Now, she only hoped Finn would continue to be patient—he had waited a long time for her after all. He could wait a bit more.

Tired of being alone with her thoughts, Poppy forced herself to dress in a dark blue dress, though she didn't wear anything underneath except her chemise, corset, and corset cover. The idea of even drawers, let alone anything else touching her blistered cheeks, was enough to make her want to cry again.

Her blonde hair was arranged in a neat braid. As a married woman, she supposed she should comb it back into a tight bun at the nape of her neck like her mother had worn hers before she died, but she was too crabby to care and they were miles away from the nearest neighbor.

She went downstairs, her nose catching the smell of bacon and eggs. She was surprised Finn could cook when her own brothers had relied on her cooking for long. Then again, Finn had been a bachelor for thirty years; perhaps, like Poppy, he had thought he would never marry.

A frown appeared on her face. She hoped Finn wasn't stupid enough to think she would be dumb enough to forgive him for thrashing her behind with a silly breakfast. He would be lucky if she didn't kill him in his sleep.

However, she was surprised when she went downstairs and found a frowning older woman in her fifties, with thinning gray hair, frying breakfast at the little stove. Poppy flinched as she pressed her back against the wall. Was it an intruder? But why would an intruder make her breakfast?

The woman finally noticed her as she placed the bacon on a plate and placed it in the center of the table for what she assumed would be for her and Finn.

"Ah, you're awake. The boss said you might sleep all morning. I don't know why. You're young and you're not birthing any babies. Wait until you get to my age and you'll know what being tired truly is. I'm just glad you're not one of those lazy women who likes spending all her time in bed."

Poppy didn't know if she should be offended or shocked at her commentary.

"Who are you?"

"I'm Ruth. Your maid-cook." Ruth started fussing over the breakfast dishes.

"What?" she asked stupidly.

"Your husband hired me. He told me to come today." Ruth glanced at her as if she were a moron.

Poppy felt a pang of hurt settle in her chest. Why would he hire a maid without consulting her? Did he think she would be a terrible housewife? Why, he had seen her take care of the Bennington house for years and she had practically raised Anthony, Iris, and Lily. Not to mention, it was their honeymoon. They should spend time together, so why was he trying to avoid that by bringing in a maid? It wasn't like the house was very big, how would they be able to have any privacy?

Maybe he had already grown tired of her. Perhaps Poppy would spend the rest of her years feeling loveless and in an unhappy marriage while she watched her siblings be madly in love with their loves. She hoped Finn would give her at least one child. Then perhaps she wouldn't feel so lonely.

"Coffee, Mrs. Weston?"

Poppy jumped when she heard herself being addressed that way. She would no longer be addressed as Miss Bennington. Poppy would be Mrs. Weston for the rest of her life. She didn't know how she felt about it exactly.

"Where is my husband?"

"In the barn, I suspect. He said he was not returning to work until tomorrow but that he still had some things to take care of outside. Call him in, won't you? Breakfast is getting cold."

Poppy felt annoyed at being ordered around in her own house. It felt like she was being reduced to a child instead of a wife.

The blonde stomped all the way towards the barn, which

was surprisingly clean. Finn was there, silently stroking his horse's mane.

"You're awake."

"Yes." Poppy crossed her arms over her chest. "And our new maid wanted me to inform you that breakfast is ready."

"Ah, so you met Ruth."

"I did. It would have been nice to get some type of warning that she was coming."

"I was going to tell you yesterday, sweetheart, but you were so terribly upset, you kicked me out of our own bedroom."

"Because you spanked me!" she hissed at him, then turned around as if afraid someone might hear.

Finn chuckled as he approached her. "Don't worry your pretty little head. There is no one here for miles. No one heard you cry and scream." He cupped her bottom in his large hand. "How is your bottom? Still sore, I hope. I have some ointment which could help reduce the swelling."

Heat rushed to Poppy's cheeks as she tried to speak without stuttering. "Why did you hire a maid? I've run a house for over ten years, I do not need a maid's help."

"I know you have been very responsible since you were only fourteen years old." Finn pushed back a stray blonde hair. She was surprised to admit how much she liked it when he did that. "Running the house, taking care of your younger siblings, cooking, and cleaning for everyone because you refused to accept the help from someone who wasn't family. Don't even try to deny it," Finn warned firmly once she opened her mouth to protest. "You didn't get to enjoy your youth as you should have because you sacrificed yourself for your family."

"I was happy to do so," Poppy mumbled under her breath.

"I know you were, but now you're married and your

priorities are different." He squeezed both of her arms. "Ruth will stay here for a month. If you want her to stay more, we can discuss it."

"I don't want her here now."

"You're overtired," Finn said firmly. He spoke to her in the way he sometimes spoke to her younger sister, Lily, which annoyed her. "You spent the last five months as a waitress to make ends meet, working from dawn to dusk. You're my wife now. You don't have to do that anymore. All you have to do now is relax."

"And what am I supposed to do with all of this free time? Ruth said you're returning to work with Chris tomorrow." Poppy tried to hide the pain in her voice, but she didn't think she was doing a very good job.

Finn shrugged as he placed a hand gently at the back of her head and started pushing her towards the house for breakfast. "Whatever you want to do. You can go shopping in town or to visit Ruby and Lucy. I just expect you to be back by dinner and before it gets dark. Don't make me go look for you, Pop. You won't like it. There's an extra horse in the barn you can use, just be careful." He opened the door and gave her a slow wink. "Now, wife, let's enjoy breakfast."

After they ate, Finn went on to continue doing his own chores while Ruth cleaned the house from top to bottom, refusing Poppy's help. Feeling like a stranger in her own home, Poppy decided to visit Ruby in town.

Finn helped her saddle up one of his smaller female horses he had named Candy—courtesy of Lily who had actually named the horse when she was quite young. Finn made her promise to come back before it became dark. Poppy had to bite her tongue to resist saying something which would just cause her to get spanked.

Her sore bottom bounced in the saddle as she made her way into town. It was a hot morning nearing the end of July, and she couldn't wait for fall. The young woman hated the heat, but of course, Finn loved it.

It felt strange having the time to herself. She couldn't remember the last time she had spent a morning doing what she desired. Of course, with Iris and Lily being older and all her brothers moved out of the house, she hadn't been as stressed as she once was when she was younger.

Iris and Lily had often complained that Poppy was too controlling. Poppy argued that she just liked keeping busy, but now, thanks to Ruth, she was alone with her own thoughts. She wasn't sure she liked it.

Unlike the other girls in town, she didn't have many hobbies, or friends she could visit. Reading and sewing bored her, and unlike Iris, she didn't want to get a job and she doubted Finn would even allow it.

It seemed she would have to find a way to keep herself occupied at least for the month Ruth would be here. Maybe she would get pregnant soon and have a baby to keep herself occupied.

Larkspur Valley had grown in the past few years, yet Poppy still felt the judgmental eyes on her when she arrived at the town square. No doubt people were starting to gossip about her arrival and how she had returned married to Finn, even though she had claimed she couldn't stand him.

It wasn't the first time the townspeople had gossiped about Poppy, but it was the first time their gossiping had made her feel small. Perhaps she wasn't as strong as she thought she was.

After putting Candy away in Steve's small barn, she smoothed down her skirts and knocked on the door of her brother and his wife's house. At least no one would bother her here, and if they did, then Ruby could practically handle them on her own. She didn't let anyone make her feel small, and Poppy had always admired her for that.

Ruby opened the door wearing a long red apron. She could see Silver playing in the sitting room with one of the rag dolls Lily had made for her from old dresses.

Before she married Steve, Ruby had been one of the most popular prostitutes in town, thanks to her beauty and spunky personality. It still surprised Poppy how she had settled down into the role of wife and mother, especially since she knew her brother was not easy to deal with.

But Ruby was in love with Steve and she loved Silver to pieces. She had told Poppy and Lucy she didn't mind making certain sacrifices if the three of them were happy together.

Ruby gave her a perplexed look. "Poppy, what are you doing here? It's supposed to be your honeymoon."

Poppy sighed as she went inside. She scooped up Silver in her arms, causing the little girl to squeal in delight. "Finn hired a maid for a month to help with the housework and the cooking. I'm bored out of my mind."

Ruby winced. "He hired a maid during your honeymoon? When you two were supposed to be together? Alone?

"Yes." The irritation grew in Poppy's voice. "Apparently, Finn can't stand the idea of being alone with me even though he was the one who insisted we marry. Maybe he has grown bored now that he married me."

Ruby shook her head. "Don't say that. The early days of marriage are awkward. I'm sure you and Finn will be able to find your way back to each other soon. He wouldn't search for you for months only to toss you aside in a few days."

"He feels sorry for me." Poppy started bouncing Silver on her hip. "They all do. Poor, ugly spinster Poppy Bennington who can't keep a man, who caused everyone to run in the opposite direction because they are frightened to death of her sharp tongue—"

"Now you stop it, Poppy Weston. You will not let the

words of the town busybodies get in your head," Ruby scolded her. "You are beautiful, witty, and hardworking. You practically raised Iris, Lily, and Anthony by yourself while taking care of a home. Finn adores you. Otherwise, why would he have remained a bachelor all these years? He was waiting for you to finally see what was in front of you. The man adores you; he worships the ground you walk on. You have just been too blind to see it. He nearly went crazy when you disappeared, but he never stopped looking."

Poppy looked at her feet. "Really?"

"Really." Ruby made her raise her chin so she could face her. "Now that things have finally settled down, he might be unsure on how to proceed. Just give it time. He never thought you would agree to marry him after rejecting him so many times."

"Well, technically, I didn't say yes," she pointed out. "But perhaps you are right and I am behaving a bit irrationally."

"You're not used to people saying no to you. Your husband might be the first soul brave enough to do it," Ruby teased.

Poppy rolled her eyes as she looked at Ruby's messy kitchen. "What are you trying to make?"

"A chocolate cake for Steve. I can't find the right recipe and Silver has been fussy all morning."

Poppy smiled. "Don't worry. I can help."

Poppy spent the rest of the day with Ruby and Silver but left before her brother came home and started questioning why she wasn't with her husband.

Finn was not in the barn when she put Candy away, but when she went inside, much to her misfortune, she saw Ruth was still there getting the table ready for dinner. Finn had just sat down when he noticed Poppy.

He quickly helped her into her chair. "How was your day with Ruby?"

"Fine. What are we having for dinner?"

"Roast beef with roasted potatoes and asparagus."

They ate dinner in silence while Ruth fussed with the messy kitchen. Poppy tried to come up with a topic of conversation, but since she and Ruby had spent all day discussing Finn, she wasn't sure what was appropriate.

"Ruth, you have outdone yourself. This roast beef is delicious."

"Thank you, Mr. Weston."

Poppy poked at her food, feeling the irritation grow. Ruth's pot roast was good, but not better than hers. If Finn ever gave her a chance to cook in her own kitchen, he would see how far superior it was.

"Mr. Weston, if it's all right with you, I will go into town tomorrow to purchase cloth to make new curtains for the kitchen windows and the windows in the sitting room."

"I like the curtains," Poppy pointed out. They were a soft blue. The same color of her eyes.

"They are worn out."

"Only a bit. They can still last for the rest of the year. We'll buy some new ones come January."

Ruth pursed her lips. "If you wish so, Mrs. Weston. I was thinking for dinner tomorrow, we could have some pork chops. My mother had a wonderful recipe—"

"My mother had a wonderful recipe too, and I will be making the pork chops, Ruth!" Poppy rudely interrupted. "Thank you so much for your services today, but they will no longer be necessary. Please leave. Now."

Finn raised an eyebrow but didn't protest.

Ruth huffed, obviously offended as she threw her dishtowel in the sink. "I have never worked for such a rude woman. Good evening to you, Mrs. Weston, and I hope we never meet again."

Poppy had a feeling she had earned herself a spanking,

but she didn't care. She just wanted to get that woman out of her house. This was *her* home. She was the lady of the house and Finn's wife, and she would make the decisions.

Finn stood up and begged Ruth to wait so he could give her a proper payment. While she was alone, Poppy picked at her food. She couldn't help but allow a smirk to form across her lips. It felt like she was finally taking control of her miserable life.

"Poppy, that was very rude." Finn returned to the dinner table once he paid Ruth for her trouble. He sat across from her and sighed as if Poppy was a troublesome pet he had to get used to. "Do you need another spanking so soon? I should wash your mouth with soap for behaving so rudely to Ruth."

Poppy shrugged as she picked at her food. "I didn't want her here, so I got rid of her."

"Poppy, you cannot get rid of people simply because you don't like them."

She ignored his tone. "More importantly, why did you hire another woman to be in the house when it's supposed to be our honeymoon? I suppose, like most men, now that you caught me, you lost interest."

"Of course not!" he growled. "I've been lusting for you for years, Poppy. Have asked for your hand more than twice. Did you really think I would just push you aside after we married?"

Poppy shrugged innocently as she took a bite of cold potato. "It's possible. Unless the one you really want is Ruth. If that's the case, then maybe I should give you two privacy."

"Poppy," he scolded. "Don't be a brat and behave please. I was trying to do something nice."

"You were trying to avoid me during our honeymoon, which was the opposite of nice. Now be honest with me, why are you trying to avoid me? Have you finally realized what a horrid wife you've gotten and you want to get rid of me?"

"I'm trying to give you space because, these past few days... no, months have been exhausting for the both of us," he exasperatedly as he rested his back against the chair. "And if I'm not with you, then it's easier to resist you."

"Resist me?"

"I am trying to be patient and not take you to the marriage bed, to avoid consummating our marriage until you are ready." He spoke the words carefully. "It's easier for me to resist you if we are not in the same room."

Poppy felt her cheeks redden. "Oh." She took a pause. "You want to lie in bed with me?"

"I do. For years now."

"Is it hard for you to wait while I'm in your presence?"

"Yes, you're beautiful, Poppy. Any man would have a hard time resisting you. However, I am the lucky one who gets to call you his wife. But I will not pressure you to truly become my wife, not until you're ready. I don't mind waiting for months." He looked at her wearily. "I was trying to be helpful. Ruth was supposed to give you a break from all the hard work you've been doing for years. I didn't mean to insult you. I know you've been an excellent housekeeper for years. I just thought you would like to relax on your honeymoon."

"I am perfectly all right. I don't like strangers in my home," she said quietly. "I am happy with it just being us."

He nodded, a slight smile on his face. "As you wish, Mrs. Weston."

They both returned to their food until Poppy spoke again. "I believe we should return to the subject of our wedding night. I think it's time we took care of it. Don't you?"

Finn looked surprised. "Yes, if you are open to it."

"Of course, I am." She picked at her food. "It is God's will, after all, and I want children. One can't happen without the other. Let's enjoy our dinner."

After dinner, Poppy quickly washed the dishes while Finn made sure the barn was locked and the animals were situated. Nerves fluttered in her belly and Poppy wanted to do nothing more than hide under the covers.

But she needed to be brave. This had been her suggestion after all. Not to mention that she couldn't expect Finn to wait forever. They needed to do their duty as husband and wife.

Even if she was terrified of the process.

It couldn't be so terrible, could it?

Lucy and Ruby were both married women and she had heard from the gossiping women in town that it was just a poke. How terrible could a poke be?

The terror must have been written on her face because Finn offered his hand and gently guided her upstairs. "Don't worry, Pop. I will take care of you. I will go slow, I promise."

Poppy took his hand and he squeezed it. This caused her to immediately relax. Finn had never harmed her before and she doubted he would start now.

Yes, he had spanked, but that was just Finn. Her own brothers spanked their wives as well, but it was never done with cruelty.

She couldn't believe she was going to become a woman tonight. She had always assumed she would have her mother by her side to teach her about the marriage bed instead of going in without a clue.

Poppy clutched her hands together, feeling extremely shy.

"Cat got your tongue, Pop?" Finn teased her gently. "I've never seen you so quiet."

"Just be gentle, please, Finn," she begged him quietly.

Finn patted her cheek. "Of course, I will, Poppy." He then leaned down and gave her a gentle kiss. His kiss was warm and soft, not like the quick kiss he had given her on their wedding day. This one was much nicer.

The kiss helped Poppy relax as she felt the stiffness of her shoulders melt away. It became deeper as he gently pushed her against the wall. His kisses traced from her plump lips down to her neck, her clavicle, and finally, towards her heavy breasts which were concealed by the large bows on her dress.

Poppy stared at him with her face flushed, as if wondering what the next step would be. His fingers slowly unbuttoned the row of buttons, exposing her chemise and, underneath it, the stiff corset with its lacy details.

Even though she didn't pull away, she stiffened. No one had ever seen her naked and she had naturally good health, so even a simple doctor's visit was out of the question. Now, the first man who was going to see her naked was going to be her husband.

Finn had seen her lower half naked, but that had been during a punishment so it didn't count. This was the real deal. Not to mention, she had always been more self-conscious about her heavy bosom over her bottom anyway.

Sensing her nervousness, he quickly landed another kiss on her lips. "Don't worry, I'll be gentle." Then her clothes were removed, and her dress, her chemise, her petticoats, even her drawers were left in a pool at her feet until she was only in her corset.

Poppy squirmed under his watchful eyes, trying to hide from view the V of the blonde curls between her legs.

"May I?" Finn touched the strings of her corset. She nodded quietly, trying to hide her blushing face.

He removed Poppy's corset and corset covers, leaving her breasts exposed, with the tight, pink nipples which became hard little pebbles the more her husband stared at them. Poppy didn't know what to hide——should she hide her breasts or the place between her legs?

Sensing her nervousness, Finn immediately started kissing her breasts. First, focusing on the top part of her breasts, then twirling his tongue over the hard, pink tips.

Poppy whimpered at the new, wonderful sensation she was feeling as her husband began sucking on her nipples. A throbbing sensation grew between her legs as she started rubbing her body against his while he played with her breasts, squeezing, caressing, and leaving behind finger marks all around her curvy figure.

"You're so beautiful, Poppy." Finn kissed her again as he squeezed both heavy breasts together. "The most beautiful girl in the world. I am beyond lucky to call you my wife. I have waited for so long for you, my Poppy."

Poppy grew pleased by the remarks as she curled her head against his neck, attempting to be petted. "Thank you for being so gentle and for making me feel pretty."

Finn growled as he placed his thumb against her chin while he squeezed one pink buttock in his hand. "You have always been pretty, Poppy. Don't forget that. How's your bottom? Do you think you will be all right if I place you on your back?"

She winced as his fingers touched the belt marks which had started to heal overnight but that she would probably wear for a few days. "Can I lie on my stomach instead?"

He nodded as he kissed her forehead, promising to place some ointment on her bottom after they were done. He led her towards the bed, instructing her to lie on all fours with her bottom raised up and her breasts crushed against the mattress.

"Open your legs, Pop. It's nothing I haven't seen before." He pushed her thighs apart, exposing her slit and white inner thighs, and with her spanked rump on full display.

She felt vulnerable with her rump in the air, but at the

same time, she couldn't deny the throbbing sensation which was growing stronger the more she stayed in that position.

Poppy had never thought she would find herself in this position. She might be twenty-seven years old, but she wasn't a complete moron, though she had always thought the man lay on top of the women during intercourse. Perhaps she had been mistaken.

Finn's finger ran through her slit, rubbing against her folds while her dewiness coated his finger. "You're so perfect, Pop. So wet for me." He entered one finger inside her which caused her to whimper. "That's it, sweetheart, the wetter you are, the easier it will be for me to enter you. It won't hurt as much."

"But it will hurt, right?"

"Yes." He tucked back a piece of blonde hair from her forehead. "It almost always hurts, but only the first time. I will try to be as gentle as possible, lovely. I promise. Do you trust me?"

Poppy nodded as she twisted her head to watch him undress. She had never seen a man naked before, and she had to admit she was a bit curious.

Gone were his stiff, worn-out looking rancher clothes, exposing a tan, muscled chest covered with dusty blond hair leading to the section between his legs. When his own drawers were removed, she sucked in her breath, feeling the redness return. She felt like she was about to faint.

Finn's manhood was large, throbbing, and seemed like it was looking directly at her. It was bright red and covered with blue and purple veins. The mushroom head of his cock was dripping a thick, white liquid.

That thing was going to be inside her?

It took all her willpower to keep her thighs spread apart even though the only thing she wanted to do was close her legs and hide under the covers. She had survived for five months on her own and yet making love to her husband terrified her. Where was the logic in that?

He rubbed her lower back in an attempt to relax her. "It won't hurt as much as you think it will, sweetheart," he whispered.

"It's too large to fit inside me!" she blurted out.

"Nonsense," he cooed as he started rubbing her clit with the pad of his finger. "Your body was made for me. You just have to trust me."

Poppy whimpered as he gave her clit a small squeeze with the pad of his fingers.

Finn positioned himself behind her, placing his hands firmly on her hips while the head of his cock rubbed against her inner thighs. Poppy stiffened in response.

Finn caressed her neck. "Shh, sweetheart. You're safe with me."

His cock started pressing against her entrance, parting her open little by little. The sensation was strange but not entirely unpleasant. He was halfway inside her when she suddenly felt a pinching sensation between her legs.

A whimper escaped her lips when she felt the pain. Finn quickly caught on and started cupping her breasts, squeezing them while playing with her nipples. Kisses covered her back to the top of her spanked cheeks.

When she was distracted with the way he was stroking her hair, he entered her fully, his manhood spreading her wide open as he took the last traces of her maidenhood. Her eyes grew wide in surprise as tears threatened to spill down.

Finn placed his hand on her chin as he turned her around to face him. He kissed her urgently, wiping the tears away as he continued thrusting into her gently so she could get used to the feeling of him inside her.

"Shh, it's over, sweetheart. The pain is over. There will be nothing but pleasure from now on. I promise."

Finn continued thrusting into her while his fingers focused on caressing the small button between her legs. Her breasts swung gently against each other. The pain was still there, but not as terrible as it was at first. It was almost enjoyable now.

"Move your hips, Pop. It will make it feel better," Finn instructed.

Poppy did as she was told, her bottom rubbing against the firm muscles of his chest. Her heart was beating faster; it was like it wanted to jump out of her chest. "Oh!" she cried out as she felt an array of sensations hit her at the same time.

Finn's warm seed coated her insides and inner thighs. It felt sticky, warm, and dare she say, pleasant?

Both of them tumbled on the bed, with Finn careful not to land on top of her. She adored hearing the sound of his labored breaths and the way his cheeks had pinkened happily. Poppy's virginal blood coated her smooth thighs and the head of his cock. She made a mental note to ask her husband to clean both of them up with a washcloth and some warm water.

Finn placed a hand on her cheek. "Are you all right, sweetheart? You're not in pain?"

Poppy loved hearing the gentleness in his voice; it was better than the scolding tone he had used on her for the past few days. "I'm fine, just tired." She didn't know how exhausting sexual intimacy could be.

Finn pressed his fingers against her eyelids, closing them. "Then sleep, sweetheart, you've earned it."

Chapter 8

POPPY WOKE with her face curled up against the crook of Finn's arm. Her face felt warm from being pressed against him.

Finn had had his arms wrapped around her the entire time. It had been rather pleasant.

Poppy hadn't been sure she would be able to sleep with someone else in her bed, but she had been delightfully proven wrong. It felt right sleeping with Finn. She'd felt warm and protected, like nothing would ever hurt her again.

She supposed that's how one must feel with a husband.

Poppy was reminded that she was naked when her breasts gently touched his muscled chest. She quickly pulled the sheet over herself.

Finn saw this and chuckled as he pressed a kiss against her forehead. "You don't have to hide yourself from me, Pop. I have seen every inch of you."

Poppy's blush deepened and she wanted to do nothing but hide under the covers even if her husband was just teasing her. They had awoken in the middle of the night and he had made love to her once more. That time it hadn't hurt as much.

Finn brushed her blonde hair away from her face. "How did you sleep?"

"Very well, thank you, and you?" The sun was up, which meant it was after eight.

"Splendid." Finn brushed his hand against her cheekbones, looking at her gently, as if he was afraid she might disappear again. "I love you, Poppy."

Poppy stared back in shock. She knew Finn had longed for her for years and he had been a close friend even when they had been at each other's throats, but she had never realized Finn might truly be in love with her. Especially when she had been less than kind over the years.

"Love?" She let out a nervous laugh. "But I've been a complete witch to you over the past few years. I'm surprised you don't hate me."

"You were hurting, not to mention dealing with a lot for a young girl. You acted like a brat sometimes, but I could never hate you." He paused then continued gently, "It's all right if you don't feel the same way right now. I am a patient man. We are going to be husband and wife for a very long time. I can wait."

Poppy wrapped her arms around Finn's torso, wondering what she had done to deserve to marry such a kind-hearted man. "Thank you for your kindness."

———

"How's married life treating you?" Christopher asked a week later, after they finished branding some of their new cattle.

"It's been blissful." Finn chuckled. "Though I'm surprised you don't already know, given that Hugh has invited himself to dinner three times this week."

The dark-haired twin was surprisingly protective of Poppy and had forced himself into their lives to make sure Poppy was happy. During last night's dinner, he finally seemed to realize Poppy was not miserable, and had stopped looking at Finn with hatred in his eyes.

Christopher laughed. "Hugh will calm down soon, but you seem happy. Calmer than I have seen you in months. For a while, I truly believed you had to be hospitalized because you were acting like a mad man."

"That was because I didn't know where Poppy was. Now I know where she is at all times. More importantly, she is mine." Finn ran a hand through his blond hair. "I'm sorry. I am talking about your sister; you probably are not interested in hearing about this."

"No, I don't mind. You've been sappy when it comes to Poppy for years. It's nice all your begging has finally come to fruition." Christopher got on his horse to head back to the ranch. "I won't get involved in your marriage, but are you two happy?"

He thought back to the past week he and Poppy had had together. Sweet kisses, nice dinners, and cozy evenings. It seemed they had finally settled into a routine, not to mention Poppy's rough edges had softened now that she didn't have to prove how tough she was.

"Very happy."

"I miss having you around. Lily is a pain. She doesn't listen," Iris complained as she pushed the sugar bowl towards her eldest sister.

Poppy added some sugar to her tea and listened to Iris' complaints patiently. Even though she had her own home now, she still felt terribly lonely when Finn wasn't around.

She would finish the morning chores quickly and spend the early afternoons with her sisters once they were finished with school or with her sisters-in-law to give them a break from taking care of their babies.

Her husband didn't mind as long as dinner was ready when he came home and he didn't have to go search for her. Poppy still had a hard time believing that she was married.

After twenty-seven years, she was finally married, and to a man who adored her, who had been standing in front of her for more than a decade. It was funny how life worked out.

Poppy couldn't remember the last time she had felt so happy for many days in a row. She usually felt like a ball of stress about to explode at a moment's notice. Finn had softened the rough edges.

"She's young, only thirteen. You weren't exactly a ball of sunshine at her age, either," Poppy assured her firmly. Though Iris had always been the calmest and more mature of the three sisters, she also had a rough temper and could be stubborn when she felt she was being wronged.

Iris pinkened. "I wasn't as annoying as she is. I can't wait until I can get a teaching job and finally have my own place."

Iris was set to graduate school next June and planned on taking the teaching exam so she could get a teaching certificate.

"You know Christopher would never allow you to leave Larkspur Valley unmarried," Poppy reminded her, her voice gentle. She knew Iris desperately wanted to be a teacher, much to her brothers' chagrin. They believed she should focus on finding a suitable husband.

Iris wrinkled her nose. "I can't teach if I'm married. Besides, Larkspur Valley is so old-fashioned compared to the larger cities. They will never offer me a teaching job, especially if the school board knows Chris is against it." She cocked her head to the side. "You left Larkspur Valley unmarried."

"Yes, and it was the most miserable five months of my life. The outside world is cruel, Iris, much more than you know. It's not as easy to survive as you may think." She playfully tugged on Iris' blonde braid. "Don't fret about it, poppet. Just focus on graduating and passing your exam. We can talk to Christopher when the time comes. I'll help you convince him. I promise."

Iris hugged her tightly. "Thank you, Poppy. I'm glad you're back. You're the only one who truly listens to me."

"Our brothers care about you as well, Iris. But they are men, old-fashioned men, and they think differently. You must be patient with them. They only want what is best. Besides, Daddy left behind some money for you in case you want to dedicate yourself to teaching full time."

Iris was quiet and demure. Unlike Poppy, who had longed to be married for years, Iris seemed content to be alone. Poppy sometimes worried for her sister, but she didn't want to pressure her to do something she didn't want to do.

Iris squirmed in her seat. "I wanted to ask you something as well. Would you accompany me to join the Ladies' Social Circle group at church? I would go on my own, but anyone who isn't married has to be accompanied by a married lady." Iris wrinkled her nose, obviously disagreeing.

"What is the Ladies' Social Circle?"

"A group made by Mrs. Simon; she asked Anthony for permission. They are planning on hosting conferences, planning charity events, things like that. Mrs. Simon is planning on bringing in interesting women speakers, which is the only reason I want to join. You know how unbearable Mrs. Simon is."

Mrs. Simon's husband owned the mercantile and was the mother of Chrissy Simon who had treated Lucy and Ruby horribly when they had first come into town. She, no doubt, was the one dragging Poppy's name through the mud about how she had suddenly returned to town married to a different man after she had been jilted at the altar.

Poppy wasn't too excited about returning to the town's social circle and she much preferred being out in the country with just Finn. But she couldn't avoid church forever, especially since her brother was the pastor. Besides, the gossip would die down once Poppy made her appearance.

"Of course, I will join you, Iris. When is it?"

"Saturday, at one in the afternoon, at the church. You don't have to go if you don't want to. I can ask Ruby or Lucy."

Poppy doubted they would go. Ruby was still considered a harlot even though she was properly married now and Lucy was terribly shy. Not to mention, they had Silver and Lloyd to take care of now.

"Nonsense. I will go with you. Finn works only half-days on Saturday. He can watch over Lily while we're at the meeting."

"I'm not five!" Lily screamed from outside where she was running around pulling at flowers to make a flower crown.

"But you act like it!" Iris screamed back.

Poppy sighed as she continued watching her sisters squabble. She was suddenly grateful for her quiet home with just herself and Finn.

On the day of the meeting, Poppy wore a demure pink and white gingham dress. Before she married, she had worn darker colors such as gray, brown, or black because they didn't get dirty often.

However, Finn had gently suggested she wear the pastel colors he loved on her so much which suited her fair complexion. Poppy thought they were impractical and too girlish. She wasn't a young girl like Iris, after all. Still, her husband had bought her the cloth of pink and white gingham as a gift for their first month of marriage. With Lucy's help, they had managed to finish it in under a week.

"I don't remember the last time I've seen you in pink." Iris smiled as Finn dropped them off in front of the church while promising Lily to take her to the candy store.

"I haven't since you were a child." She smiled when she thought about how her husband had looked at her. Finn's eyes had widened with glee before he spun her around the room until she told him she was growing dizzy. "I forgot how much I liked it. Maybe it's why I dressed Lily in pink so much when she was a baby."

"It suits you."

"Thank you."

They sobered when they entered the church. Anthony waved from the last row of pews where he was speaking with the men who were going to put the new church bell up in a few weeks.

The ladies of the group were all gathered in the first couple of pews. Mrs. Simon, of course, was in the center, where the rest of the ladies gathered around her like hungry birds. Poppy saw a few of Iris' friends sitting down, looking miserable. No doubt they had been forced to come by their mothers.

"Go join them." Poppy squeezed her hand. "I'll be fine."

Iris thankfully did as she was told. The last thing she needed was for her little sister to overhear any comments the old bats might make of her.

Mrs. Simon finally stopped talking when she noticed her. She walked towards her with brisk steps. "Ah, Miss Bennington. How nice to see you again."

"Hello, Mrs. Simon. My name is actually Mrs. Weston now."

Mrs. Simon's beady eyes went towards Poppy's wedding rings. "Ah, yes, I heard that you married your brother's helper."

"Yes, Finn. I'm happily married now." She didn't like the way Mrs. Simon spoke of Finn, as if he were a servant. Finn had proudly been her brother's right-hand man when none of her brothers wanted to go into ranching. He was a kindhearted, hard worker and she wouldn't let Mrs. Simon insult her by making it seem like she'd married beneath herself.

"Congratulations. So sorry we couldn't attend the wedding, yet neither could your siblings and their wives." Mrs. Simon gave her a toothy smile. "Mrs. Weston, Poppy dear, I was wondering if I could speak to you in private."

Poppy retuned the smile. "Anything you would like to say to me, Mrs. Simon, you can tell me right here."

Mrs. Simon winced, but her smile didn't fade. "All right, dear. I didn't want to say this in front of Iris, but if you insist."

"Just say it, Mrs. Simon."

"I was wondering if there was anyone else who could accompany Iris to these meetings. Perhaps Mrs. Ruby Bennington, or better yet, Mrs. Lucy Bennington. She has such fine sewing skills which will surely be helpful."

"What is wrong with me? Though I do agree, my sewing is not as impressive as Lucy's."

Mrs. Simon winced. "Miss Bennington—"

"Mrs. Weston."

"Mrs. Weston, the other ladies and I believe you are not the best representation for our little group. We want to serve as an example for the town about what a good Christian woman should be."

"And you are an example of a good Christian woman?" Poppy scoffed. "Judging before you fully know me? Isolating me?"

"This is a respectable group." Chrissy Simon stepped forward, placing a hand on her mother's shoulder. "We do not need to hear your story. Everyone in this room knows what you've been up to, Poppy Bennington. Getting rejected by three men in your lifetime. Running around Wyoming unsupervised. Returning, married to that worker. I'll be surprised if there wasn't a baby cooking in your belly with an unknown father—"

Poppy pounced on her before she could finish insulting her. She didn't care if Finn tanned her hide. Chrissy had insulted her and her sisters-in-law for years. She had always ignored her, but now she couldn't. Not anymore.

Chrissy shrieked as she fell to the floor while her mother screamed for help. The ladies looked around with a stunned expression as if they were watching two monkeys fight. Iris was struggling to contain her laugh as she winked at her sister.

Poppy tugged on Chrissy's hair. "Why are you such a hateful, vile woman? I'm surprised you don't burst into flames every time you step into a church."

"At least I'm not a shameless little whore!"

Thump.

Chrissy screamed as she touched her bleeding nose. "Oh, my nose! My poor nose!"

"Someone help my baby!"

Poppy felt someone grasp her by the waist, pulling her away from Chrissy. Anthony stood red-faced behind her as she tried to squirm away. "What is wrong with you? Why are you acting like a child?"

"She started it!" she protested childishly.

"Well, I'm ending it," Anthony growled, looking angry,

which was a rarity for him. "Wait in my office, Poppy, until I come get you. We need to have a talk. Iris, stop smiling and go retrieve Hugh. Here, Miss Simon, let me help you up. Ladies, please exit the church. Your meeting will have to happen at a later date."

Poppy looked over her shoulder, praying that she had broken Chrissy Simon's nose.

Chapter 9

"YOU NEED to learn how to control her," Anthony mused as he closed his Bible before he stared at Finn. He looked exhausted—no doubt, he had been dealing with the women of the community and their husbands during the entire afternoon.

Hugh had informed him of Poppy's afternoon scandal when he reached him, Christopher, and a group of other men who had been rounding up the cattle to finish off the day. He had been partly amused, partly irritated that he had to make the journey to the Bennington ranch to tattle on his twin sister, though he had looked proud of the fact that Chrissy Simon had received what she had coming to her. She had been a pain ever since Lucy came to town to marry Chris.

Finn looked around the empty church. He supposed he should be grateful his wife hadn't broken the windows or mauled the girl half to death. She and Hugh had awful tempers, even worse than Ruby, who had simmered down a bit after her daughter's birth.

"It's not about control," he sighed. "She's not a puppy. I can't have her tied to a leash all day. She'll go crazy and then she'll take it out on me. Poppy needs to learn how to curb her temper and think before she acts, I agree, but her behavior needed to be corrected years ago. Now she's used to doing what she likes and I don't know how to school her differently."

"Our father spoiled her," Anthony agreed. "And Poppy had to learn to be independent from a very young age. Perhaps you can teach her how to ask for help when she's overwhelmed and to turn the other cheek when someone hurts her. Our Heavenly Father will take care of any misdemeanors."

Finn shook his head. "Easier said than done. Sometimes a smacked bottom is the only way I can make Poppy understand when she's done something wrong."

"Well, it's a good thing her brother is the sheriff. I doubt many would cross her," Anthony joked.

"How is Miss Simon?"

"She will be all right. Hugh patched her up, nothing broken thankfully, just a bruised lip and a bruised nose. Her father isn't pleased. He owns the mercantile so it will be best if we don't upset him."

"I will take care of Poppy. Thank you for taking her back home. I know it's a bit of a trip from town. She wants to ride everywhere, but I don't like letting her out of my sight."

Anthony nodded, looking pleased that he was being protective of his older sister. Poppy had held tightly to the reins when it came to running the Bennington home. Now it was time for someone to take care of her.

When Finn arrived home, the house was quiet, though he could smell something cooking on the stove. Roast beef, his favorite. The little hellion was probably trying to get into his good graces after she got into a fight at the church.

Well, he was not going to let her get away with this so easily. Finn was holding a switch in his hand. Before he had come into the house, he had picked it from a nearby tree, carefully cutting off any leaves and splinters. He didn't want to make her bleed, after all, only make his wife sore enough that she would think twice next time she decided to act like a lunatic.

"Poppy!" he called out.

When she didn't answer, panic entered through Finn's body. What if she had run away again? Would she really run away because she knew she deserved a spanking? "Poppy!" he called again.

With a hurried panic, he checked the tiny kitchen, the storage room, and then the basement. When he didn't find her there, he checked upstairs, his chest growing tighter by the second. He wouldn't be able to handle it if she had run away a second time.

Finn let out a sigh of relief when he found his wife curled up on a settee, fast asleep, her little hands curled into fists. He wondered if there would ever be a time again when he wasn't worried she was hopping on a train or stagecoach.

Poppy looked adorable curled up in the chair. Finn wanted nothing else but to pick her up and make sweet love to her, but she had behaved very naughtily today. She needed to know that there were consequences. He was not going to be a husband who let her get away with everything like she had done in the past.

Poppy Weston was a wife and, hopefully, would be a mother soon. She needed to start acting like it.

After she took her punishment, there would be plenty of time to cuddle and soothe her.

Finn supposed he should let her sleep. They'd both had a very long day after all. However, another part of him told him he should take care of this indiscretion sooner, rather than later, so they could both move on.

Poppy would try to act cute and wifely tomorrow, to get herself out of a punishment, and Finn's need for her was so great, he quite feared he would let her get away with murder.

No, the sooner he got this punishment over with, with a clear head, the better.

"Poppy," he said her name again. Poppy didn't stir, but he saw her nose twitch.

The little brat.

"Wake up." Finn clicked his tongue. "I know you're faking."

Poppy sighed as she sat up. "I'm sorry, all right?"

"Sorry is not good enough." Her husband shook his head. "Poppy, what possessed you to attack Chrissy Simon in the middle of a ladies' meeting? You could have injured her severely. Just because your brother is the sheriff, does not mean you can go around injuring people who upset you."

"She deserved worse than what I gave her," Poppy murmured.

"Poppy!"

"Sorry," she grumbled, but she didn't sound very sorry.

"Why did you do it?"

Poppy bit her lower lip before she started to stubbornly look at the floor. "Poppy."

"She was being mean to me and rude and just awful. Chrissy Simon is a terrible person. She didn't treat Ruby or Lucy with any respect when they first came here. Even though I am married now, she is acting like I'm some unwanted floozy—"

"That is still no reason for you to behave like you did. You could have seriously hurt her. If Chrissy Simon acts unladylike, you simply ignore her or you let me know and I will speak to her father, but what you don't do is act like a lunatic. You are a married woman now, Poppy, and I expect you to act like a lady at all times. Is that understood?"

"Yes," she grumbled under her breath.

"Yes, what?"

"Yes, sir." Poppy glared at him. "You have been awfully bossy lately. I didn't know you could be so bossy and stern. If I would have known, I would have never married you."

"Yes, you would have," he teased her as he brushed his thumb against her plump bottom lip. "And I didn't know you were so adorable. You do know we have to take care of this little incident, right?"

Poppy's shoulders slumped as she looked at the switch in his hand. "I know." She paused. "At least it's not the belt."

Finn laughed. "Don't tempt me." He used the switch to point to the bed. "Bend over the bed, Poppy. Place two pillows under your hips to raise your bottom. I don't want to hit anything besides your tush. Let's get this over with and move on to more pleasant endeavors."

She blushed a bit, knowing what he meant by that as she slowly made her way towards their bed. Poppy draped herself over the pillows, raising her bottom up.

He could tell she was nervous because she was squeezing both of her hands while her eyes glistened with unshed tears. Finn was torn whether he wanted to punish her or not. She had only acted like she had in defense of herself.

But if he let this slide, then Poppy would never grow up and think twice about her actions.

Finn pushed up her skirts and pulled down whatever was covering her rear end from being properly chastised by the switch. When her bottom was bare, he gripped the switch in his hand before placing it against his wife's bare bottom.

"You're getting twenty-five lashes." Poppy whimpered. "Count them."

The switch was raised in the air before landing on her

rear end, leaving behind a pale pink line. She practically jumped. "One."

The switch landed again, this time just below the first mark, resulting in an identical pink mark. "Two."

The switch landed firmly against her bottom multiple times and then the backs of her thighs, covering the area with a multitude of switch marks and pink welts which would become itchy as they healed.

Poppy cried out after each lash, her cheeks bouncing gently against each other as she was punished. Every once in a while, she parted her pale thighs, exposing her creamy pink quim which was growing wet with her dewiness. She might not like getting spanked, but her body certainly did.

Her round cheeks trembled with the anticipation of another stroke. Her butt was covered with an array of at least a dozen switch marks ranging from pink to red. Finn landed one final stroke between the center of both cheeks.

"Twenty-five!"

Finn dropped the switch and began rubbing his wife's bottom. His large, calloused palm was caressing the tender skin as he tried to be careful with the sore welts. Poppy whimpered when she felt his hand touching her welted ass cheeks.

"It's all right, sweetheart. It's over," he soothed her. "You did really well, honey."

"It hurt," she whimpered hoarsely as she turned to stare at him with bright blue eyes.

"I know, baby, but it's all over." Finn placed his hand between her legs and started stroking her wet quim, focusing on the little bundle of nerves.

Poppy stiffened slightly when she felt his thumb grazing her clit before she started moaning, rocking her hips to the rhythm of his fingers. He loved hearing her moan. It brought nothing but joy hearing her cry out for him.

"I'm sore," Poppy protested as he pushed her on the bed.

"I know, sweetheart." He traced his tongue against her inner thigh. "But I'm going to make you feel good right now. I promise. No more punishment."

His fingers grazed the buttons of her dress as he started undressing her, ripping apart every inch of clothing until his wife was fully nude. He would never tire of looking at her, of smelling her sweet scent and hearing her sweet cries of pleasure.

Poppy shielded her plump breast from him, still feeling a bit shy even though they had been married for over a month now.

Finn gently pried her hands away. "Don't hide yourself. I want to see every beautiful part of you, my wife."

Poppy blushed but did as she was told. He removed all of his clothes in order to better appreciate his wife. His cock was hard and standing at attention, desperate to bury himself in her quim.

Poppy raised an eyebrow when she saw how needy he was for her. "Maybe I should be naughty more often."

Finn growled at her as he cupped one spanked buttock in each of his hands and pulled her towards her edge of the bed, until her lower half was dangling from the edge. He knelt down, getting a full eyeful of her quim covered in dusty blonde curls.

He pressed his mouth against her slit before using his tongue to coat every nook and cranny of her womanhood. His wife squirmed, obviously embarrassed as she tried pushing his face away, but he quickly put a stop to it by squeezing her whipped cheeks.

Poppy quickly forgot about her embarrassment when she started enjoying the way he was pleasuring her with his tongue, making sure his heavy tongue didn't miss any part of her. He sucked her plump little lips, giving them gentle bites which caused a shiver to go down his wife's spine.

He parted her lower lips slightly with his tongue to get better access to the small bundle of nerves between her legs which caused women to scream out in pleasure. He spent the next fifteen minutes sucking on her clit and giving it teasing licks until he was sure his wife was close to losing herself.

Finn quickly got up and buried his cock between her legs in one quick thrust, catching his wife by surprise. He smirked when he saw the look on Poppy's face as he started making love to her in slow, sweet strokes.

He then grabbed her by the waist and pulled her up so that her legs were wrapped around his waist while she was still impaled on his cock. "Ride me, sweetheart," he whispered in her ear.

Poppy smiled as she did as she was told, moving her hips like he had instructed her in the past and rubbing her body against him. Poppy's pleasured cries filled their bedroom as she met her needs.

Breathing heavily, he placed her gently on the bed, making sure this time she was on her belly instead of her backside.

Poppy wrapped her arms tightly around him, pulling him closer as she snuggled her cheek against his chest. "I'm tired."

Finn kissed her nose. "Then let's get some sleep, lovely."

Thirteen years ago…

"Shh, shh, Lily, don't cry." Fourteen-year-old Poppy bounced her newborn baby sister against her hip like she had watched Mother do a dozen times with Anthony and Iris. "Please, please don't cry."

The begging only seemed to cause her baby sister to cry even harder. Baby Lily was a cute baby when she was awake and giving everyone toothless smiles, but when she was upset, she turned into a red faced, screaming, boiled cabbage looking thing who liked pulling on her own golden strands of hair to get attention.

Usually, Poppy was able to calm her down by rocking her to sleep or cooing to her. This time, however, she wasn't sure what was wrong with Lily. She had helped Mother take care of Anthony and Iris when they were babies, but she had never been fully responsible for one.

She felt quite hopeless. A lady from church had suggested the baby might have colic when she had heard her crying at church, but Poppy wasn't exactly sure what colic was and she was too proud to ask. Most women in town already thought she was too clueless and too young to be able to take care of a baby properly.

Poppy would not give them the satisfaction of proving to them that she couldn't do it.

Anthony pressed his hands against both ears. "Make her stop! She's been crying for hours; doesn't she get tired?"

"I'm trying," Poppy snapped, trying not to yell at her little brother, but it was hard when she was dealing with a crying baby, Iris holding onto her skirts, and the idea that she still had to prepare dinner.

"Why is Lily crying?" Iris asked innocently.

Poppy wasn't sure. Her diapers were clean, she wasn't sick, and she made sure she had the freshest cow milk in her belly after she convinced Father not to hire a wet nurse or a nanny. Poppy didn't want any strangers in the house after Mother's death.

"Pop, where are we going?" Anthony whined.

"To see Chris. He'll know what to do."

Sweat clung to her shabby dress, and the pink ribbon which was barely holding her hair up was close to slipping. She knew she looked a mess, but between the cooking, cleaning, and taking care of the baby, she hadn't had time to properly take care of herself like she used to do. Her father had stopped insisting they hire a maid or a housekeeper when he saw how upset she got by the suggestion.

Worst of all, the majority of her dresses no longer fit. They were too snug in the hip area and the buttons across the bust were always threatening to burst open. Mother had talked about letting down her skirts to hide her ankles and getting dresses more appropriate for a young woman. Mrs. Bennington had died before being able to take her to the dressmaker and she was too shy to go herself.

Poppy breathed a sigh of relief when they finally reached Christopher's bachelor house. It would be easier to have gotten there by horse, but she wouldn't be able to ride with Lily, Anthony, and Iris. She made a silent note to ask Steve how to attach the horse to the family's wagon.

Christopher had mentioned he was going to talk to some new hire from Virginia, hopefully they were done by now.

Dragging her siblings behind her, she pushed the door open without bothering to knock. "Chris—"

She stopped short when she saw Christopher speaking to a young man who was a few years older than she was. He was handsome, with neat, though patched, clothes, tidy blond hair, and a friendly smile.

Poppy had never thought about courting before. Father had mentioned she couldn't until she was sixteen, but every time she thought about the man she would marry, a man like the one in front of her appeared in her mind.

The baby crying brought her back to reality and made her realize how silly she was being. With her dirty clothes and limp hair, not to mention lackluster personality and awful temper, there was no way a man like him would want her as his wife.

It would be better for her not to get too excited, but a part of her, a small part of Poppy Bennington, hoped that when she would marry, it would be to a man exactly like him.

A man with blond hair and kind eyes.

Chapter 10

"WHAT A HORRID GIRL Chrissy Simon is. She must be the devil's daughter. How can so many horrible things come out of her ugly little mouth?" Ruby said with sympathy as she gave Poppy a slice of vanilla cake. The frosting was melting and the cake appeared dry, but Poppy stuffed it in her mouth. She didn't want to be rude.

Lucy and she had been trying to teach Ruby non-stop how to cook, but the blonde always managed to burn everything. Her brother must have an iron stomach to be able to eat Ruby's cooking. Though Steve was so in love with Ruby, he would probably eat pig slop if she asked him to.

Poppy hadn't been in town for the past week. Her husband told her it might be better if she stayed behind at the ranch instead of going into town, to wait for the gossip about how she had punched Chrissy Simon to die down.

She doubted that would ever happen, especially since Ruby had gossiped to her that it was all anyone talked about ever since the incident happened. Chrissy Simon hadn't shown herself at church, but her mother used every opportunity to bad mouth Poppy, even though Chrissy wasn't exactly well-loved or respected.

Finn allowed her to visit Ruby after he was tired of her complaining about how bored she was, with the promise that she wouldn't go frolicking in town, which Poppy thought was unjust. Finn pointed out he wanted to make sure she returned in one piece.

Ruby's eyes shone with mischief every time she told the story, since she couldn't stand Chrissy and she wished she had done it herself. Poppy was often reminded how young Ruby was, only twenty. It was no wonder Steve had a hard time managing her at times.

As the oldest, Poppy often tried to do her best to sound demure and be the voice of reason, but when she was around Ruby, she felt like a girl again. She hadn't had many friends growing up, even less when Mother died. She hadn't even finished school properly, even though Father had wanted her to. Poppy hadn't wanted anyone else in the house. When she was around Lucy and Ruby, she was transported back to her school days.

Ruby elbowed her in the ribs. "Come on, laugh. I know you want to. Don't give me a lecture. You and I both know Chrissy should have been given a slap in the face ever since she was rude to Lucy when she married Chris. You don't have to be so uptight all the time. Tell me again, how did her face look?"

"Like a piano fell on top of her. Horrid girl."

"Good. It's a pity you didn't break her nose." Ruby smirked when she saw Poppy was struggling to eat the cake. It felt like she was eating sand. "You don't have to eat the cake anymore. I know it's disgusting."

Poppy pushed the cake plate back. "Then why are you still letting me eat it?"

"Because you and Lucy are too nice to say anything. I

know my cooking is horrible. The only one who eats it without complaining is Steve, and that's because he would eat hay if he was hungry enough. I hope Finn wasn't too harsh. Steve would have tanned my hide for a month if I had pulled such a stunt, and in his brother's church no less." She gave an exaggerated sigh. "He is so strict with me."

Poppy rolled her eyes. "He is not. You have him wrapped around your little finger, Ruby. Don't even complain. You've gotten away with more stuff than most."

Ruby tossed her blonde hair over her shoulder. There was a smile on her pretty lips which reminded Poppy how beautiful she was. Before her brother had gotten her pregnant with Silver, Ruby had been the most expensive whore in Larkspur Valley, known for her beauty.

When Poppy had first met Ruby, she had been jealous of her beauty and how men had looked at her. The only man who had ever looked at her like that had been Finn, and while she adored her husband now, at the time it felt like the universe was mocking her.

Now, after getting to know her sister-in-law better, she was no longer jealous, especially when the blonde could be funny and mischievous. Her daughter was heading in the same direction.

"The punishment wasn't so bad. Nothing compared to when Finn dragged me back into town. It was just a switching." A switching which had left behind pink and red welts that had been itchy for days. She blushed when she remembered what happened after the switching.

Lovemaking could be so wonderful, she wondered how Finn and she managed to leave the bed sometimes. She had heard from other women growing up that performing her duties as a wife was a horrid and painful chore, but so far, she had enjoyed every minute of it.

"Why are you blushing when I mentioned your

punishment?" Ruby teased her. "Did something happen? Tell me! Steve has come home so tired lately that he is not fulfilling his duties as a husband. Or have you and Finn already become a boring husband and wife?"

Poppy wrinkled her nose. "I don't want to hear about my brother in that capacity. Besides, what Finn and I do in the privacy of our bedroom is none of your business." She tried to sound firm, but she was shaky at best.

Ruby squealed as she pulled her into a hug. "Oh, Pop, I am so happy you and Finn are getting along. More importantly, you are happy. Lucy and I were worried, well, that you two would end up killing each other one of these days."

Poppy laughed softly. "We wanted to in the beginning, believe me, but somehow everything is less complicated now. He listens to my needs and I listen to his. It's strange, I admit it, but it's like two pieces of a puzzle coming together. I'm happy now, more than I would ever have been with Richard."

"That is so romantic. Especially knowing how Finn has been fluttering his eyelashes at you for years." Ruby placed a hand on her cheek. "Did you love Richard? I know you were humiliated when he left you on your wedding day, but were you sad or embarrassed?"

"Embarrassed, mostly," she admitted. "I wasn't in love with Richard, but I was already a spinster. I didn't want to remain unmarried and childless while the rest of my siblings found love. It sounds silly, I know, but I was feeling incredibly lonely at the time. Perhaps Richard and I would have never fallen in love, but he would have been a companion. At the time, I thought that would be enough."

"And now?"

"Now I wonder why I was so stupid. I didn't see what was inside of me."

"But you saw it just in time. Finn loves you, Poppy. I may not be as sappy as Lucy, but I can tell you how much he adores you. He was running like a fool for months."

Poppy chuckled. She was still too embarrassed to say the word "love", feeling like a schoolgirl when she did, but that's what she was feeling right now. Complete and utter love.

"Ruby, I wanted to ask you a favor. Could you help me?"

"Gladly."

Poppy fumbled with her hands, not really sure how to bring up what she wanted to ask Ruby. She knew what she was about to ask from the blonde was nothing out of the ordinary. She would probably be honored that she had asked.

Still, Poppy felt like a silly schoolgirl approaching the popular girl in school.

She had thought about asking Lucy for this favor, but like Christopher, Lucy was sensible. While her appearance was always tidy and presentable, Lucy wouldn't consider herself a fashionable woman.

Besides, like Poppy, she was a rancher's wife. She couldn't dress as if she was going to Sunday service every day, still, Poppy wanted to feel pretty at least every once in a while.

Ruby snapped her fingers in front of her. "What did you want to ask me? I know that look on your face. You are about to take back whatever it is you wanted to ask me. Don't. Just tell me."

"I was wondering if you would help me to be prettier. If you wouldn't mind." Poppy cleared her throat, feeling the blush rush to her cheeks.

Ruby cocked her head to the side. "What do you mean? You are pretty. Anyone would love to have your long blonde hair and blue eyes."

"I know I am not hideous, but I am plain. I'm the oldest of the girls. I never had a mother or an aunt to teach me about these things. I just wish I didn't look so uninteresting. Can you help me?"

Ruby squealed in delight. "Of course, I will. I love fixing myself up. The only one who wants to talk about hair and clothes is Lily but, of course, she's too young. It will be nice to talk it over with another woman. Iris and Lucy are not really interested in clothes."

"I just don't want to look so plain," Poppy whispered, "so invisible. I don't want Finn to regret marrying me when there are so many girls in town who are prettier and younger."

Ruby slapped her hand lightly in a scolding way. "Don't put yourself down in front of me. You are lovely, Pop, you just need my expert hand to make yourself even lovelier. Don't forget, Finn has been obsessed with you since he first laid his eyes on you. You could wear a potato sack and he would still love you."

Poppy removed her hair from her bun, letting her golden hair cascade down her shoulders. "What should I do about my hair?" She had never cut it before and it reached below her knees. While she got many compliments on it, it was heavy. She sometimes envied Lucy's short brown curls that reached the top of her shoulders. Her hair had never really grown back after she sold her hair to purchase a ticket to Larkspur Valley to marry Christopher.

"Maybe cut it. I think it would look good at shoulder level."

"Finn would redden my rump if I cut it so short. Maybe halfway down my back, a little longer than Lily's hair. What do you think?"

Ruby nodded as she grabbed a pair of scissors. "Perfect. What do you think about bangs?"

"I never tried them before. Do you think they will look good?"

"You have an oval-shaped face. Bangs always look good on oval-shaped faces."

Ruby grabbed a fistful of blonde hair.

"Do you know what you're doing?"

"Yes. You learn other things besides bedding strangers when you live in a whorehouse. Now stop moving. I want to finish before Silver wakes up from her nap."

Poppy tried her best not to squirm even though shivers went down her spine every time she heard Ruby's scissors move in the air. She hoped her sister-in-law didn't ruin her hair; otherwise, she wouldn't be able to do anything but cry.

"Done. You look perfect if I do say so myself. Maybe I should open my own place."

"As if my brother would allow you to return to work."

"It can be like a secret club, only for women. What Steve doesn't know won't hurt him."

"Your bottom will surely hurt after he's done with you."

"Stop being so sensible. Now open your eyes." Ruby shoved a mirror in her lap.

Poppy opened her eyes, widening when she stared at her reflection. Her blonde hair was a little shorter than she had asked, above her breasts, but it didn't look as terrible as she had thought it would. Soft, blonde bangs were across her forehead.

"You look cute." Ruby pinched her cheek. "I know it's proper to have it up in a bun, but you can always add flowers or ribbons so it doesn't look so plain."

"Won't it look childish?"

"No, it's feminine. Now, for clothes." Ruby raced up the stairs and returned holding a soft green dress with pale yellow flowers. It was a beautiful dress. It looked expensive. When Ruby had been working as a prostitute, she had bought herself many expensive clothes.

"Here. I want you to have this. Take it."

Poppy shook her head. "No, I can't take your dress. It's yours. You spent so much money on it. I can just wear some of my old stuff."

She wrinkled her nose. "No offense, Pop, but your clothes are boring and matronly. This is much better. Maybe we can convince Finn to take us to Laramie when spring comes. They have such nice stuff, much better than Larkspur Valley. Take this for now, I insist. Wear it to church on Sunday along with your new hair. Place your bangs back so Finn doesn't notice."

"But it's your dress."

"It doesn't fit me anymore." Ruby sighed. "I purchased it before Steve and I married. My breasts and hips expanded after I gave birth to Silver, but you came back to town as thin as a rail. It might be a bit tight in the chest, but nothing you can't fix, just make your corset tighter. Now take it. I won't take no for an answer."

Poppy clutched the dress to her chest. "Thank you, Ruby."

She winked. "Anytime. You deserve to be happy, Poppy."

The following Sunday, Poppy dressed carefully in her new gown after the breakfast dishes were done. Thankfully, Finn was busy hitching the horses to the new buggy he had bought for them recently in preparation for the winter months.

The dress fit like a glove and she made a mental note to buy green more often. It was a little tight around the chest, but nothing that was noticeable. She braided her hair like Ruby had taught her to do, though it came out sloppier than she'd wanted. She twisted the braids into a small bun at the nape of her neck and tied a green ribbon around it. Her bangs brushed softly against her forehead, making her blue eyes look bigger.

She nervously placed her sweaty hands against her skirt

as a hundred questions popped into her head. Would Finn like her clothes? Would he think she looked lovely or silly? Would he be proud to have her on his arm as they arrived at the church today?

"Pop! Hurry up, we're going to be late," Finn called out.

"C-coming."

Poppy made her way downstairs, her skirts brushing against the stairs as she made her way down. Her throat felt tight as she reached the bottom of the stairs and faced her husband.

Finn stared at her, his eyes widening with surprised pleasure. "You look—"

"All right?" she asked nervously.

"Better than all right, you look beautiful." Finn wrapped his arms around her waist and pulled her close. His cock brushed against her lower belly and she wanted nothing else but to take him upstairs so he could ravish her. "And your hair is shorter. It suits you."

"Does it really? I wanted you to like it."

"Do *you* like it?"

"Well, yes. Ruby does have a trick or two up her sleeve. I wanted a change. I was ready for one. I never had time to put too much time into my appearance, but I finally do. I thought it was time for a change."

"If you're happy, then I'm happy, Pop. You make me a proud husband." He squeezed her shoulder. "Let's go to church. I can finish fawning over you later."

The church service felt long even though Anthony always managed to develop witty sermons. The only thing Poppy could think of was how much she wanted to be with her husband.

After the service, Lucy, Ruby, and the babies gushed over her while her brothers teased her like they always did.

Her heart jumped inside her chest when Finn said the magic words, "Let's go home."

Finn and Poppy arrived home in record time, both already knowing what to expect. Poppy teased Finn about how it was a miracle that he hadn't broken their new buggy by how fast he was going.

"You looked stunning today," he praised as he led her inside.

"Really?"

"Like an absolute doll, Mrs. Weston." He placed his hands around her waist then led her to the dining room table where he instructed her to lie down with her back against the table. "Spread your legs, honey."

Poppy did as she was told, her neck and cheeks turning bright red as she spread her legs open.

Finn pushed aside her frilly underthings and spread apart her drawers, giving him access to her womanhood.

"You're so wet for me, honey," he teased her as he ran a finger down her slit. Poppy shivered.

Finn kneeled down, placing both hands on the backs of her thighs as he started pressing his face between her legs.

His wife started squirming as she remembered the last time he'd done this. "What on earth are you doing?"

"Tasting every inch of my wife." He smirked as he teased her with his tongue. The tip of it swirled near her clit, parting her dewy lips to reach the little nubbin between her legs. "Every." *Lick.* "Sweet." *Lick.* "Inch."

"Oh, that feels wonderful, Finn," she whispered as she clutched pieces of her dress to keep herself from screaming. "Keep doing that."

"I thought you didn't like it," he teased.

"I was wrong." Finn sucked on her plump, inner folds. His lips caressed the soft lips as she squirmed on the table. "Please, Finn, oh!"

Finn spent the next few minutes pleasuring her, making sure he caressed every part of her with his tongue until she was a wet, trembling mess. He allowed her to orgasm once before he unbuttoned his trousers, releasing his long, thick cock.

He entered her swiftly in one quick swipe. Poppy moaned as she felt the sudden fullness between her legs as he pounded inside her.

Her husband squeezed her buttocks, grabbing one round cheek in each hand as his cock slid in and out of her. Poppy's breasts heaved inside her tightly corseted gown, threatening to spill out.

Their hips rocked against each other as she felt his hot seed spill inside her. Finn slapped one of her buttocks, leaving behind a pale pink handprint. "Good girl, Poppy."

Poppy whimpered as she raised herself up slightly and rubbed her face against his chest, wanting to be petted.

Finn grunted as he placed himself on top of her, both of their chests heaving up and down. Finn pressed his lips against her neck. "I love you so much, Poppy."

"I love you too," Poppy whispered.

Finn's eyes warmed up. "Truly? You don't have to say it if you're not ready."

She loved the way Finn looked at her with complete adoration, like he was looking at a queen.

"No, I'm ready. I love you, Finn." Her voice crackled with nervousness. "I love you so much, darling. I'm glad I married you. I don't think I have felt this happy in such a long time."

Finn smiled as he stroked her hair. "I don't think I was happy until I married you."

Chapter 11

"I'LL SEE YOU TONIGHT." Finn kissed her forehead as she curled her head against his neck wanting to feel his warmth. It felt like she had barely gotten to see him during these past few days. "I'll be late again tonight. You don't have to keep dinner warm for me. A simple sandwich will do."

"Finn." She shook her head. "You're going to work yourself to death, especially if you are not receiving proper food. Can't my brother ask someone to stay behind? Someone who doesn't have a lonely wife at home?"

Steve and Chris also worked long hours to provide for their families, but at least Lucy and Ruby had their babies to keep them company.

"Three men have been sick with influenza and two men returned west because they couldn't handle our Wyoming winters anymore." He pinched her cheek when he saw she was not satisfied with the answer. "Oh, come on, Pop, don't be angry with me. Give me a smile. It's only for a few more weeks. You don't want the cattle to die from the cold, do you?"

Poppy pouted. "What am I supposed to do while you are at work all day?"

"You could find yourself a hobby." Finn kissed her again, leaving her behind to think about what her hobby could possibly be.

The rest of the morning, Poppy thought about potential hobbies. She had never had so much free time before. Since she was used to taking care of a larger household, preparing meals and cleaning didn't take as long as it usually did.

Poppy thought all that morning about a potential activity she might enjoy. She didn't like reading, not even when she had gone to school. She wasn't particularly good at watercolors, and although she was good at sewing, she wasn't as talented as Lucy with a needle and thread.

Then she thought about her mother. She had been a beautiful, dainty woman who reminded Poppy of Lily, especially as the youngest Bennington grew older. She had loved flowers so much, she had named her daughters after her favorite flowers. Mrs. Bennington had kept a beautiful garden which had been the envy of the townspeople.

It had sadly wilted in the aftermath of her mother's death as everyone was too sad or too tired to care very much about flowers.

Poppy perked up. Maybe she could revive it. She had never done much gardening before, perhaps now was her chance. She quickly got up and grabbed some of her pin money that Finn gave her every week, grabbed her horse, and went into town.

Thankfully, there was a small store which sold packets of seeds at expensive prices near the church. Poppy had been afraid she would have to go to the mercantile which was run by Chrissy's father even though the man was much more pleasant than his wife and daughter.

Using her pin money, she bought three packets of seeds, a pair of gardening gloves, a small gardening kit, and a tiny watering can, which could barely hold enough water for a glass.

When Finn returned home from work, he found his wife on the side of their house, elbow deep in the dirt despite the freezing temperatures.

"You're going to catch your death," he scolded as he pulled her up. "What on earth are you doing, Poppy?"

He landed a smack on her upturned rear which caused her to squirm away from his punishing hand.

"Gardening."

"It's too late in the year to garden. Everything you plant will die before it even blooms properly or the seeds will slip out from where you planted them due to the rain."

"You told me to find a hobby."

Finn sighed. "I know, but I thought you would choose something more sensible, like reading or making quilts. Gardening when it's so close to winter, it's not practical, darling. I don't want you roaming around at all hours in the cold."

"I know, but I wanted to try the new tools I bought and just have everything ready once spring came." She smiled. "My mother had a beautiful garden before she passed. Maybe I can create one that is half as beautiful."

If her husband thought she was being silly, he didn't comment. Instead, he simply kissed her, even though both of them were covered in dirt. "I'm sure it will look lovely, sweetheart. Now, let's both get inside and have a hot bath."

Winter was coming soon. Finn could feel it as the wind cracked down against his skin when he returned home.

Christopher had left work early, in order to spend the evening alone with Lucy, much needed after the birth of their son. Lloyd would be spending the evening with him and Poppy, along with Silver, whose parents had also wanted some alone time.

Finn smiled when he arrived home and saw his wife playing with their niece and nephew. He had stopped scolding her for being outside after sunset. Poppy was a country girl through and through and she hated being cooped up inside.

Poppy was chasing Silver, who had barely started to walk, around as she pretended to be a monster who was trying to catch her. Silver was moving her chubby legs as fast as she could, and Finn was surprised she hadn't tripped. Silver was squealing in delight as she watched Poppy chase her.

Baby Lloyd was lying down on his belly giggling in delight as he watched his cousin and Aunt Poppy run around.

Finn went to put his horse away in the barn then picked up Lloyd who snuggled against him. He loved spending time with Silver and Lloyd. They were adorable and they made his baby fever spike.

He couldn't wait until Poppy was pregnant, but he didn't want to pressure her about a baby yet. They had only been married for a few months after all.

"What are you little rascals doing?"

"Playing, playing, Finny!" Silver squealed as Poppy finally caught her.

"Got you. Now, let's get you cleaned up so we can sit down for dinner."

"Toast! Toast!"

"Not toast. Chicken and mashed potatoes." Silver pouted. "And if you're good, I'll give you two cookies."

The mention of cookies brightened Silver up as she went willingly with Poppy to get her hands washed.

"You're a natural," Finn whispered in her ear as she cleaned Silver's hands with soap. "With both of them."

Poppy chuckled. "You're not so bad yourself." She poked Lloyd's cheek as he was squirming in Finn's arms.

"Do you want children, my love?" he asked as Lloyd managed to free one of his little arms from his grasp. "I don't mean to pressure you, but when I see you with Lloyd and Silver, I find myself desperate for our own babies."

She laughed as she started drying Silver's hands with a hand towel while the little girl squirmed. "Of course, I want babies—in due time, of course. They will come."

Finn kissed her.

Poppy blushed when she realized they had an audience.

Lloyd started whining, obviously not liking being squished.

Silver stuck out her tongue.

"How many do you want?"

"Two. Maybe three. Certainly not seven. But I think three will be a nice number."

Finn chuckled as he placed a hand on her lower back. "Three it is."

As he helped Poppy get the dining room table ready and the children down to eat their supper, he couldn't help but imagine their own little family they would hopefully one day have.

Finn couldn't wait until that day.

The next morning, Finn and Poppy first dropped off Lloyd with Lucy and Christopher then they headed into town to drop off Silver with her own parents. Both couples looked pleasantly exhausted as they thanked them for taking care of their children before they added they would one day happily return the favor.

"Christopher asked me for some things to bring to work on Monday." Finn helped her out of the wagon. "Can you entertain yourself for an hour or so? We'll meet back here and then we can enjoy the rest of our Saturday. Perhaps we can have a picnic."

Poppy nodded eagerly as she picked up her little drawstring purse. "I'll buy more seeds."

"Enjoy, honey, but don't waste all your pin money on seeds. Not until the spring."

Poppy headed to the little shop she had gone to last time. She was still avoiding the larger mercantile store even though the entire Simon family had been avoiding her like the plague since she returned to the church.

"My, aren't you a busy little bee." Mrs. Ingraham, the old lady who ran the shop, chuckled when she saw her come in. "Coming for more seeds, Mrs. Weston?"

"Yes. I was looking for pumpkin seeds."

"Pumpkin seeds will not be ready to be planted until late summer, young lady. You best try planting cucumbers or tomatoes if you want something you can eat in the spring."

Poppy nodded as she went to the back of the store to look at the little packets of seeds. They were expensive, but as Mrs. Ingraham had mentioned, she had to send for them. In a few years, when her garden had settled, she would be able to use their seeds to plant new ones.

Finn thought it was odd she wanted to start planting food when, originally, she was only going to plant flowers, but she thought vegetables might be more fun. Not to mention, they were more useful than flowers.

Poppy looked at the seeds carefully, wondering which ones would be more practical to buy. She did love pumpkin flavored food, but Mrs. Ingraham was right; she would have to wait almost an entire year to eat pumpkin and they might not take root.

She sighed, then picked up the small envelope labeled cucumber.

"Poppy?"

Poppy felt a chill go down her spine. Mrs. Ingraham hadn't mentioned there was another customer in the store, but then again, the old lady spent more time talking to herself than looking at her surroundings.

She recognized the person who had called her name. Poppy almost wished that the one who had done so had been Chrissy Simon. She was surprisingly more tolerable than the alternative.

Poppy slowly turned around. Perhaps her brain was playing tricks on her. There was no way that man had come back to haunt her. Not after she had cried about being humiliated for days. Not when she was finally married to the love of her life.

Not now.

Poppy thought that when she saw Richard again, she would have been filled with hatred and anger, reminded of how she had been left on their wedding day. Instead, she felt a familiar, throbbing sensation in her throat as if she might cry any second now.

Every inch of Poppy wanted to hide so Richard didn't see her anymore. She felt small under his gaze. Small and insignificant, though she should thank her lucky stars that her brothers weren't with her at the moment. Otherwise, they would surely end up killing him.

Her eyes widened when Richard stood in front of her. He had never been handsome, but he had a pleasant look on his face that had won Poppy over.

A different Richard stood before her now. It looked like he hadn't shaved in weeks and stubble covered his cheeks. There were dark circles under his eyes and his hair looked disheveled.

"Richard," she whispered, hoping no one was able to hear her. The last thing she needed was for busy bodies to hear and go blab to her brothers, or worse, her husband about Richard.

"Hiya, Pop." He gave her such a sad little smile, she almost felt sorry for him. "How are you doing, darling? Is life treating you well?"

"Is that all you have to say to me?" she hissed. "After you left me at the altar, might I add."

"I know, I'm sorry." His voice crackled. "Please don't be angry."

"You're lucky I am not slapping your face," she hissed as she crossed her arms over her chest. "What are you doing here? When did you come back?"

For her sanity, Poppy knew she should run in the opposite direction, but she needed answers. She needed to know why Richard had left her on their wedding day when everything had been going fine.

"I came back last night. I only came for one day, to finish collecting my stuff, mementos, and all. After that, I am leaving Larkspur Valley for good." He swallowed. "Can we talk? Please."

Poppy hesitated. Finn wouldn't be happy that she was talking to Richard, but she also felt bad leaving him standing there so pathetically.

"Fine. Five minutes, but not here."

"Fine. Let's go to the back of the store. Outside. It's still early."

"Five minutes," Poppy repeated. "I mean it, Richard, not a minute more. My husband will be looking for me."

A wry smile appeared on his face as he looked at her wedding band and engagement ring. "You married?"

"Yes, five months after I was supposed to be your wife. Finn Weston."

"Your brother's right-hand man? Finn's a good man."

"Yes, he is."

"Poppy, you changed your hair. It looks lovely."

"Richard?"

"Yes, Poppy?"

"Shut up."

Chapter 12

POPPY KEPT LOOKING over her shoulder as if she expected Finn to pop out from under the bushes. She really hoped her husband didn't see her meeting with her ex-fiancé. Finn would be so hurt, not to mention, what explanation could she come up with for giving Finn another chance after he humiliated her in public?

But a part of her needed to hear Richard out. Maybe once she knew why he had broken her heart, she would be able to make peace with the whole thing. Lucy had once told her that one day she would be able to laugh about her misfortunes. She hoped the brunette was right.

"Well, I'm here. Talk." Poppy crossed her arms over her chest.

He cleared his throat. "Well, first, congratulations on your wedding. Finn is a good man who will surely take care of you. Are you happy?"

"Very. We are planning on having a baby soon."

Poppy didn't know why she was telling her ex-fiancé this. Perhaps to rub some salt in the wound. However, if Richard was upset, he didn't show it. Dare she say he almost looked relieved, as if a big burden had left him.

"Good for you. I'm sure your babies will be adorable. You will be an excellent mother, Pop. Both Iris and Lily adore you. I'm sure your children will too."

"Thank you," Poppy responded begrudgingly. It was hard to resent someone who was being civilized when there was no lost love between them, even if he had humiliated her on her wedding day.

Poppy had agreed to marry Richard because she had wanted a family and a husband, and Richard, well, she wasn't sure why he had agreed to marry her. Especially when he had been planning on leaving her at the last minute.

"Where are you living now?" Poppy asked once the silence became too much. She wanted to end this conversation. The longer she took, the more she ran the risk that someone would find them.

"Salt Lake City."

"That's quite far from here."

"It is, but I left so abruptly that I left some belongings I couldn't part with."

"Why did you leave?"

"Pardon?"

"You heard me. Why did you leave?" She raised her chin defiantly. "The church had been booked. Half the town had been invited. I spent weeks making my wedding dress. You were the one who proposed to me. Why did you leave me behind as if I were a dirty sock? I deserve an answer."

"Of course, you do, honey. Please lower your voice." Richard looked around nervously. "Poppy, I am so sorry I caused you so much pain. You are a kind girl, a sweet girl, and you didn't deserve what I did to you. I should have stopped it sooner, but I didn't know how. Not to mention, your brothers would have torn me limb from limb if I broke the engagement. They can be quite scary, especially your twin."

Poppy stared at him in disbelief. "You would rather leave in the middle of the night like a common thief before facing my brothers? Believe me, they were more angry on the day of the wedding than they would have been if you would have broken the engagement properly."

Richard looked away, obviously embarrassed, but he didn't deny it.

She couldn't believe she had ever planned on marrying such a coward. She couldn't imagine her husband running away from any type of situation even though Richard had a point, her brothers could be quite intimidating.

"I couldn't marry you, Pop," he said carefully. "You have to believe me. I didn't do it to be cruel. I did it for your own good. You wouldn't have been happy married to me. I tried to break it off before it went too far, but you wouldn't let me. You kept trying too hard to prove yourself to be a good wife. Not to mention, you were stubborn. I kept hoping you would change your mind after I gave you the ring, that you would see we weren't right for each other. But the wedding date came sooner than I expected and it was too late. It was like stopping a runaway train. Impossible to stop."

Tears threatened to spill down her cheeks, but her pride was too big. She refused to cry for this fool. She already had enough regrets caused by him. She did not need another.

"I didn't realize I was such a burden," she snapped. "What would have been so terrible about marrying me? I would have been a good wife to you. I would have tried so hard to make you happy."

Poppy hated how desperate she sounded, but his rejection had hurt. especially since Richard had been the third man who had courted her and whom she had thought she would marry.

"I know you would have, honey." Richard's voice had grown soft as he looked at her with pity as if he couldn't believe such a simple-minded fool was standing in front of him. "But I wouldn't have been a good husband for you."

"Why not?"

"Because," Richard hesitated as if he didn't know what to say, "I am not like other men. I shouldn't even be telling you this. This is not something a lady's ears should be hearing. You've been brought up right. You're too sensitive."

"I have more sense than you give me, Richard. Now tell me."

"I wasn't born right. Not like other men you see. Not like men should be." He fumbled with his words, unsure on how to proceed. "Not how God dictates men should behave."

Poppy frowned, growing more confused by the second.

Richard ran a hand through his dark hair. "I feel the same way you feel about men." Poppy still looked confused. "What I am trying to say is that what most red-blooded American men feel about women, I feel about men. Men want to be with women. I want to be with men."

Richard gave her a rueful smile, as if he had taken the last bit of pie at a function.

What he was saying finally seemed to click in Poppy's head as she turned a bright red. "Oh. I don't know what to say." She felt awkward. Poppy had never heard of such a thing. It seemed almost impossible to her. Could a man really love another man the same way a man was supposed to love a woman? "I'm sorry, I just never heard of such a thing."

"It's not surprising," he said wryly. "You are a lady. I'm sure your brothers and husband kept you from hearing such things."

This was not what Poppy had expected Richard to say. She had been expecting him to say that he had fallen in love with another woman or that he had left because Poppy's dowry hadn't been as big as he had expected, since Father had left most of his money to Christopher so he could keep running the Bennington ranch. With him confessing his secret, her anger towards him had diminished a bit.

In fact, Poppy wondered how she could be so foolish. The clues that Richard had not been interested in her had been there since the beginning. When they had been courting, Richard had always kept his distance. The most she could hope for was a polite kiss on the cheek. He had never been overly affectionate, either, as one would be to a sweetheart. He had been perfectly friendly, but nothing more.

Maybe it had been a blessing in disguise that he had left her after all. Otherwise, she would have never found happiness with Finn.

"Thank you for letting me know. I hadn't been expecting that."

"It is not something I often share." He shrugged awkwardly. "I could get into a boatload of trouble if anyone were to find out my secret. Please, don't tell anyone. Not even Finn."

Poppy was not in a habit of keeping secrets, especially from her husband. But Richard looked so lonely and pathetic, she felt like she had no choice but to agree. Besides, this secret did not affect Finn at all.

"Do not worry, Richard, your secret will be safe with me."

"Thank you, Pop. You have always had a kind soul, no matter what the people in town said. Now, you realize why I couldn't marry you? It wouldn't have been a very happy marriage on either of our parts. You deserved better, Poppy. Someone who could love you like a woman should be loved. Not just as a friend. I am truly sorry for the pain I caused you. I should have been braver, but I wasn't. Now, the only thing left to do is apologize."

"Thank you for apologizing." Poppy's shoulders relaxed. She was glad this conversation was over. It felt like a huge weight had been lifted off her shoulders. Maybe now, she could get rid of this huge chip on her shoulders which had been there since she had been deserted on her wedding day. "Are you returning to Salt Lake City?"

"Yes. We will probably never meet again. I had to sort this out. Otherwise, my conscience would not have let me rest. Thank you for listening." He offered his hand. "Goodbye, Poppy Bennington. I wish you nothing but happiness."

Poppy shook his hand. "Thank you, Richard. I wish you the same wherever and with whomever you are."

A rare smile crossed his face as he tilted his hat and left. Poppy followed a few minutes later, smoothing down her dress and returning to the town square.

She flinched when she felt someone grab her wrist.

"Where have you've been?" Finn frowned. "I have been looking for you everywhere. They told me you left the store."

"You scared me." Poppy whacked him on the shoulder, trying to calm her beating heart. "They didn't have what I wanted so I thought I would start looking for Christmas presents for Lloyd and Silver."

Finn looked at her empty hands. "You don't have anything, either."

"They didn't have anything I liked enough for them."

Poppy felt guilty lying to Finn, but she didn't know how to bring up Richard without Finn becoming jealous. A jealous Finn often became irrational. Besides, she had sworn to Richard she would keep his secret.

Finn gave her a funny look. "Perhaps we'll take a trip to Laramie. Maybe we'll find better presents in the city."

"Perhaps you're right." Poppy felt itchy in her high collared dress. She suddenly wished she were back in her cozy home in the country and not in this town where she could feel everyone had their eyes on her. "Let's go home, Finn. I want to prepare a nice dinner for you and it could take hours."

Finn smiled at her. "What's the occasion, honey?"

"No occasion." She softly brushed her hand against his back. "I'm just feeling grateful today."

"For?"

"For us."

"Dinner was delicious, honey. You really outdid yourself. If I keep eating all you're feeding me, my clothes won't fit by next summer." Finn gave his wife a playful smack on her rump as she cleared away the dinner dishes.

"Good thing I am an expert with a needle and thread," Poppy teased him back.

Finn wrapped his arm around his wife. "Leave the dinner dishes and let's go upstairs, honey."

Before Poppy could answer, there was a knock on the door. Finn groaned as he went to answer the door.

On the other end, was Poppy's twin brother, smoking a cigar and looking at him with a moody expression on his face. Finn wondered why he was always so miserable, especially when the rest of his brothers were relatively cheerful.

"Finn," he greeted calmly. "Evening. May I come in?"

"Of course, but put out your cigar. Your sister doesn't like smoke in the house."

Hugh rolled his eyes but did as he was told.

"Hugh!" Poppy squealed as she went to hug her brother. "What are you doing here so late? Is everything all right? Have you eaten? I can heat up some food for you."

"One question at a time, Pop." Hugh smiled. "I already ate."

"Your dinner always consists of a piece of bread and a glass of whisky."

"It's still food. I didn't come to chit chat. I came to speak to your husband."

"Finn?"

"Yes, there's something wrong with my horse and I want him to look at it. I placed him in the barn. Finn?"

Poppy looked confused, especially since Hugh could have asked Steve, who lived in town, or Chris, who lived closer to town than Finn and Poppy. Not to mention, Hugh was a rancher's son, and even though he was a doctor, he knew more about country life than most people.

Finn quickly caught on that Hugh wanted to talk to him in private. He wondered why. He and Poppy had been married for months now and he thought Hugh had finally started to accept him.

Finn raised an eyebrow but didn't question Hugh in front of his sister because it was clear he didn't want Poppy to be nosy. "I'll take a look." Finn kissed Poppy on the nose. Hugh rolled his eyes as he murmured something about how he didn't want to see his sister receive physical affection.

"Are you finally going to punch me for daring to marry your sister all those months ago?" Finn demanded once they were at the barn. Pepper, Hugh's horse, stood munching on hay, perfectly fine.

"No. Though I still think Steve and Christopher let you

get away with marrying Pop too easily. I am not here because of that." Hugh's face darkened. "I came for something else."

"What?"

"He's back."

"Who's back?"

"Richard."

The amused look on Finn's face disappeared. Why had Richard returned months after he had humiliated Poppy? Was he determined to get her back? He was going to have to kill him first before he even got a whiff of his wife. Richard had hurt Poppy once, he was not going to allow him to hurt her again.

"What is he doing back?"

Hugh shrugged. "He left some stuff behind when he ran for the hills on his wedding day. He must have returned for that."

"He would risk a beating from you or your brothers just for material possessions?"

"He has always been a sentimental fool. I've never liked him for Pop, but she was happy. I wanted my sister to be happy, even though it's clear she makes poor decisions when it comes to men."

Finn ignored the comment which had obviously been meant for him. "Did he come back married to another woman? Did he return to beg Poppy for another chance?"

"Who the fuck cares what his reasons are? I just want to give him a lesson for hurting my sister. He might have gotten away once, but he won't again. I spoke to Harold at the station. The jackass purchased a one-way ticket on the train tomorrow. I came here hoping you would like to join me for some good old-fashioned revenge."

"Do your brothers know about this?"

"Yes, and they have given me their blessings. However, they have chosen not to get involved since they are now in full domestic bliss. They said their wives won't appreciate it." He raised an eyebrow. "What about you, are you scared of your wife too, or would you care to join me?"

Finn wanted nothing more than to break Richard's nose, especially when he remembered how much Poppy had cried when he found her. But then he thought about Poppy. She wouldn't appreciate it if he sought revenge.

Sensing his inner thoughts, Hugh pressed himself against the back of the barn. "I saw them today."

"Saw who?"

"You wife and Richard, talking in town. I was on my way to talk to Anthony when I recognized Poppy. Imagine my surprise when I saw her talking to Richard instead of you, her beloved husband. Behind one of the stores, might I add. Seems they wanted their privacy."

Finn swallowed. He had been looking for Poppy this morning in town. Had she been with Richard that whole time? What had they talked about? Would Poppy run away again and leave him here like a complete fool?

"Did they kiss?" Finn hated asking the question, but he needed to know. He trusted his wife, but he certainly didn't trust Richard.

"No. They seemed to have had a short conversation before they parted ways. Friendly, from what I saw. Still, you wouldn't want Richard to leave town thinking he can speak to your wife whenever he fancies, right?"

Finn knew Hugh was baiting him. The man loved conflict and he had gotten into so many fights during medical school, Christopher had had to spend a lot of money so he did not get kicked out.

Yet, the idea that Richard had seen Poppy behind his back, and worse, that Poppy had not said anything irked him. He felt a stab of jealousy in his chest no matter how irrational he was. How dare Richard seek his wife after he had humiliated her and caused her to disappear in shame for months?

And what about Poppy? She had told him she loved him, but what if her old feelings had returned once she saw the bastard again?

God had sent Richard back onto his path to finish what he wasn't able to last time. Perhaps he should take it.

"Well?" Hugh grinned, obviously knowing he had won. "Are you coming with me to defend your wife's honor? Stop looking at me like that; we are not going to kill the guy, just rough him up a bit so he can feel exactly what Poppy felt when he broke her heart."

"Fine. Not a word to Poppy, though."

"I wouldn't dare upset my sister. Just tell her you are going to the saloon with me and to go to bed."

Finn nodded as he returned home where Poppy was removing her apron. She smiled at him, causing Finn to clench his jaw. What else was his wife hiding from him behind her sweet face? Poppy had never lied to him before. Why did she have to start now?

"Did Hugh leave?" she asked as she wrapped her arms around his neck. "Do you want to go upstairs to bed or we can read in the sitting room for a bit. I can start a fire."

"I can't." He pulled away from her hug abruptly. "Hugh asked me to go to the saloon with him for an hour or so. Do you mind?"

"No. I'm sure Hugh gets lonely now that Steve and Chris have their families. Anthony doesn't drink so I suppose he just wants some company. Do you want me to wait for you?"

Finn looked at her innocent blue eyes and the way she was looking at him adoringly. To think that she was probably looking at Richard the same way earlier made him sick to his stomach.

Poppy was *his* wife. His. Not anyone else's.

Richard would have to walk over his dead body himself to see, let alone talk, to Poppy again.

Poppy frowned. "Are you all right? You're rather quiet. Hugh wasn't being rude, was he?"

"No." Finn touched her cheek. "I'm heading out. Don't wait up."

Chapter 13

"WHERE IS HE?" Poppy murmured as she looked at the clock. It was half past ten and there still wasn't any sign of her husband. Finn usually wasn't a big drinker which meant it was Hugh's doing that he was being kept out at all hours.

She was going to kill her brother. Just because Hugh was single and had all the time in the world to be out at all hours visiting whorehouses didn't mean he had to drag Finn down with him.

The more time passed, the more irritated she grew. Finn should be here in bed with her, not hearing some floozy sing at the piano.

The idea of a whore flirting with Finn filled her with rage even though she knew Finn was a gentleman.

The door finally opened and Finn came in. Thankfully, he looked sober. Her eyes widened when she saw his fists told a different story. They were bruised, swollen, and there was some dry blood on them.

She knew her brother wasn't happy that she had married Finn because he thought he had forced her, even though she had told him various times she was happy with her decision. Poppy had thought Hugh had gotten used to the idea.

From the looks of it, not. Honestly, boys could be such imbeciles at times.

"What happened?" Poppy raced towards him, her anger forgotten. She held his hands in hers as she studied them. She was surprised there wasn't anything broken. "Did you and Hugh get into a fight? I told you he's a mean drunk."

"Why didn't you tell me you saw Richard today?" His voice was dry, cold. But Poppy recognized the hurt tone in his voice.

"What?"

"Why didn't you tell me you saw Richard today?" he asked with gritted teeth. "Or were you planning on keeping it to yourself all along? Don't even bother lying to me, Pop. Hugh saw you two talking."

Poppy cheek reddened. "I was going to tell you."

"Were you, or were you going to take the secret to your grave? We don't keep secrets from each other, Pop." Finn started walking towards her until she was cornered in the back of the room. "What did you two talk about that you needed to do it in private? What else are you hiding?"

Poppy bit her lower lip. "He just wanted to apologize. He was sorry he embarrassed me."

Finn looked like he didn't believe her. "Was he convincing you to run away with him?"

"Of course not! Don't be silly. He's living in Salt Lake City now. He has no interest in returning to Larkspur Valley. Not to mention, I am married to you. I love you."

Finn still had a hard look on his face. "Why didn't you tell me you saw him if it was as innocent as you say?"

"Because I knew you would get like this. Blinded by jealousy," Poppy said quietly. "He apologized and he left, that is all. Why don't you tell me what happened to your hands? You and Hugh weren't drinking. Did you two fight?"

Finn clenched his jaw. "Yes, but not each other."

It took Poppy less than a minute to realize what he was saying. "You and Hugh beat up Richard. Why?"

"What do you mean why? He humiliated you. You ran away because of that fool."

"You're the fools!" she hissed. "I never asked for revenge. I've moved on from being left at the altar. Why can't you?"

"Because I remember how much pain that bastard caused you. How you left Larkspur Valley for five months. He not only caused pain to you, but to your entire family, and me. You might have forgiven him, Pop, but I didn't. I never will." He gave a humorless laugh, "Don't worry; he's not dead. He is going to be in a lot of pain when he returns to Salt Lake City, though."

Poppy gripped him by his shirt. "You are such an idiot, Finn Weston! You could get yourself arrested. Do you think I want my husband in jail? Why are you listening to Hugh, anyway?"

Finn pulled himself away from her grip. "Thankfully, your brother is the sheriff. We outnumber him, Poppy. He's just going to run home with his tail between his legs." He touched her wrist. "I thought you would be happy. I did it for you, honey."

"Well, I am not happy." Tears threatened to fall down her cheeks. "And I'm not happy about how you accused me of cheating on you because I talked to Richard in private. I would never do that to you. I thought you trusted me. We cannot have a happy marriage if you are going to fly into a jealous fit of rage every time a man talks to me. I believe in you, so I expect you to believe in me."

Finn looked ashamed. "Poppy, let's just go to bed. You're overtired—"

"I'm not overtired. I don't want you in my bed tonight, Finn. You can sleep in the sitting room or in the guest room, but you will not sleep in the same bed with me because I don't agree with what you and Hugh did. Next time, don't get advice from my brother."

"Poppy."

Poppy ignored him as she raced upstairs and locked the door behind herself. Finn followed, but Poppy was faster.

"Poppy!" Finn growled. "Open the door now. Unless you want me to rip the door open. This is our bedroom and you cannot kick me out!"

"Well, I am! I told you I don't want you here, Finn. If you break down the door like a caveman, I won't forgive you. You already have done enough for tonight, don't you think so?"

"Honey."

"Just leave! I don't want to talk to you anymore."

She heard Finn sigh as he walked downstairs.

Once she was sure he had left, Poppy slid down to her knees and did the one thing she felt like doing.

She cried.

Chapter 14

POPPY SLAMMED a bowl down on the kitchen table as she started cracking eggs over it. She then grabbed a wooden spoon and started mixing them so hard, she was surprised the spoon hadn't broken. She didn't know why she was even making breakfast. Finn deserved to go hungry.

Poppy didn't know where her husband was after she had kicked him out. He had probably slept in the guest bedroom on the floor, was probably now in the barn, or had gone in early to help Chris, which meant she was making all of this breakfast he wasn't going to eat.

"Damn him." She sucked on her finger when she accidentally cut herself after slicing a piece of bread to toast.

Her anger had only diminished somewhat since last night. She couldn't believe Hugh and Finn had acted like complete cavemen and attacked Richard. Of course, Richard had deserved a bit of retaliation for humiliating her like he had, but he didn't deserve to be beaten.

Poppy wanted to nip this kind of behavior in the bud. Her husband was sweet, kind, and protective. She didn't need him to turn into some kind of lunatic whenever he felt threatened. It would end up landing him in jail, even though Steve would probably look the other way.

She didn't want Finn to turn into a caveman like her brothers, with the exception of Anthony, though she had a feeling they were more alike than he let on.

While Poppy pressed a washcloth to her injured finger, she heard the front door slam. She turned around quickly like an angry cat. "Well, it's about time you return for—"

She stopped short when she saw her brother, Christopher, standing there looking both amused and perplexed. "Chris."

"Good morning, Pop. Judging by your angry tone, I assume you found out what your husband and twin did last night."

"Of course, I did. I would think you would be the voice of reason in preventing them from doing something so foolish."

"I told them it was a reckless thing to do."

"But you didn't try to stop them."

"No. Richard had it coming, for making you seem like a fool in front of the entire town. I don't care what his reason was, I still remember the pain he caused." Christopher playfully pinched her cheek. "Steve and I have wives and babies; otherwise, we would have joined them."

"Four against one isn't fair," Poppy said flatly.

"Neither is two against one, but Richard should be grateful we gave him some advantage. You're mad at Finn, huh? Lucy told me you would be, but I can never tell with you."

"Of course, I'm mad." Poppy stomped her foot. "He was acting like a fool, completely filled with jealousy and not thinking things through. That is not the reasonable man I married."

Christopher laughed. "Finn is reasonable except when it

comes to you, Poppy, you should know that by now. Besides, Richard has always been a sore spot for him. You are lucky you didn't marry him, or who knows what he would have done."

She rolled her eyes. "Is Richard going to press charges?"

"To whom? Our brother the sheriff, the one who is family to the two people who beat him up? Of course not; he finished any business he had in town and left. Good riddance."

Poppy scoffed as she starting placing the eggs in a pan. "What are you doing here, Chris? Did Finn send you to convince me to forgive him? It won't work. I am still mad at him."

The amused smile left his face. "He's not here? That's the reason I came. He promised to come and help me early this morning. I assumed he slept in."

Poppy blushed. "He wasn't with me all night. I kicked him out of our bedroom."

Christopher groaned. "Poppy, you don't kick your husband out when you're angry."

"What else was I supposed to do, allow him back into my bed when he was acting like a fool?" She bit her lip. "Do you think he's hurt?"

Christopher shook his head. "Let's not get ahead of ourselves. Finn is responsible, he probably went somewhere to clear his head." When he saw that his sister was not comforted by the proposition, he continued, "I'll grab my horse and go look for him. Don't worry, Pop, I'm sure he will be fine. Just keep breakfast warm and don't go outside. We don't need two fools running around."

Poppy tried to keep herself entertained by finishing breakfast then getting started on her daily chores, but she couldn't help but feel that something was wrong. Finn was very responsible and he treated Chris like a brother. There was no reason for him to skip out on work unless it was truly terrible.

She got her answer when she was throwing away the cold breakfast. Poppy had been trying to keep it warm, but it had turned mushy. She could always make something fresh once Finn came back.

The front door opened, only this time, instead of seeing her husband and Chris, she saw her twin. Hugh walked towards her, not bothering to greet her as he placed one hand on each shoulder.

"Poppy, you must promise me not to throw a fit."

"Why would I throw a fit?"

"Promise me, Poppy."

"Fine, I promise. Now what is it?"

Poppy heard the stomping of feet as Steve and Christopher came through the door, each helping the other to hold an unconscious Finn.

Poppy screamed when she saw him. There was blood spilling from the back of his head and a large bruise forming on the side of his forehead.

"Poppy!" Hugh scolded.

Poppy tried to get ahold of her husband, but her brothers were already taking him upstairs. "What happened to him? Why is he injured?"

"Stop getting hysterical." He gripped her arm. "Chris and Steve found him lying down about three miles from here. It seems like he was thrown off his horse. Steve found a dead snake nearby. The horse must have stomped it after it bit him. It must have been spooked."

The tears were coming down fast and Poppy was surprised she was still able to speak. She couldn't be a widow. Not when she was finally happy. "Is he dead?"

"No." Hugh's voice softened. "Nothing seems to be broken except perhaps a couple of his ribs, but he definitely has a head injury. I don't know how serious it is. I won't know until I examine him. Can I trust you to keep your nerves under control until then?"

Poppy nodded.

"Good girl. Just relax, Pop. Finn is as stubborn as you. He will never leave you. Not this soon."

Poppy hoped with all her heart Hugh was right. Finn had been in her life since she was a girl of fourteen. She didn't know if she would be able to survive without him.

Chapter 15

FINN FELT like he had been kicked by a horse, which was something that had happened to one of his younger brothers when he was two. The doctor had told his mother he had been lucky he had survived. All Finn remembered was that his brother had complained a lot. At first, he had thought he had been exaggerating how bad the pain was, but apparently he had not.

He flinched when he felt something cold touch his cheek —it felt like he was being touched by an icicle.

"Finn. Finn... Finn."

He squinted. Who was calling his name? The voice sounded girlish and in pain. She was close, but also far away.

The scent of vanilla and violets hit his nose. His wife's scent.

Poppy.

He had had the honor of smelling her sweet scent ever since they became husband and wife. It was a scent he wouldn't easily forget.

Finn's eyes fluttered open and he found himself staring at his wife's face. Her face was even paler than usual, her eyes swollen and blotchy, and she was gripping the bed covers as if she wanted to rip them apart due to her nerves.

Her shoulders slumped with relief when she saw he was awake. "Finn, you woke up!" She wrapped her arms around him tightly. Her embrace hurt, but there was no way in hell he was going to tell her that. Not when he and his wife were finally embracing again.

Hugging in pain was a much better alternative than how they had been screaming at each other earlier on.

It hadn't been the first time they fought harshly, but the first time as husband and wife, which had made it more painful.

"Pop, stop crying. I'm all right," he ordered her gently as he pressed a hand against her cheek which was covered with tears. Poppy had never been much of a crier, but it seemed around him, she was crying constantly. He wasn't sure if that was a good or bad thing.

"Poppy, you're slobbering all over him." Hugh, who seemed to have appeared out of nowhere, pulled his twin away. "Give him time to breathe, or do you want to injure something else?"

Poppy shook her head, looking like a lost child. Finn wanted to smack Hugh for being so insensitive with his sister even though Poppy had been hurting him a little.

"I'm sorry, Finn. I am so, so sorry. I didn't mean... I didn't want to yell at you. It's just I was so confused about Richard—"

Poppy started crying again and tears were spilling down her cheeks, much to Hugh's annoyance, who simply gave her a handkerchief.

His heart fluttered at the idea that Poppy was crying for him. It just childishly confirmed she was over Richard, which was something that caused him an infinite amount of joy.

"It's fine, Poppy, don't cry. I don't want to see you cry."

He especially didn't want to hear that bastard's name come out of her mouth again. He didn't want to spend the rest of his life in jail, or worse, hanged for his crimes, or he would have killed Richard just to be sure he didn't have contact with Poppy ever again.

"You heard him." Hugh scowled. "Now, go to the kitchen to prepare him some tea and a bite to eat so I can examine him properly. I won't get much done if you're crying all the time."

Poppy nodded, but she looked at Finn for confirmation, something which pleased him. He gave her a little nod which was all his wife needed to go down to the kitchen. He hadn't realized how hungry he was until Hugh had mentioned food.

"You didn't need to be so rude." Finn accepted Hugh's help as the younger man helped him sit up. Finn winced as he sat up slowly with his back pressed against the wooden bedframe. He definitely felt like he had been kicked by a horse now.

"She's been crying non-stop, and it's been driving me crazy. I'm a doctor, not a miracle worker." Hugh huffed as he started pressing his fingers against Finn's neck to check for swelling before inspecting the back of his head for any bumps. "I finally had to give her a tranquilizer and had her spend the night with Chris and Lucy because she was spending all her time here acting like the Grim Reaper."

Finn winced when Hugh pressed a hand against the back of his head where he felt the swell of a bump against his hand.

Hugh didn't bother apologizing. He might be a good doctor, but he had a poor bedside manner.

"How long was I out?" He continued wincing when he started patting his chest and ribs which were heavily bandaged.

"Five days." Hugh grimaced. "I wanted to take you to a

hospital in Laramie. I wasn't sure if you had any brain swelling or if you had any more severe internal injuries. At the end, Chris and I decided to have you heal here so you could properly rest. Though I would like to take you into the city to get some more tests done when you are feeling up to it."

"That won't be necessary." Hugh didn't look convinced but didn't protest. "Is anything broken, or worse?"

"No, you are a very lucky man. It's a miracle you didn't break your foolish neck. Apart from severe bruising on your back and bruised ribs which should feel better in a few weeks, you are completely fine. In about a month, you should be completely normal and back to work."

"A month?"

"Don't worry, Chris will pay you to stay home and rest. Lord knows he has overworked you to death ever since you started working for him."

"He's a good boss. It's not about the money. Just what on earth will I do at home all day?" If he could constantly be between Poppy's legs, then it would be a different story, but right now he could barely move without screaming.

Hugh shrugged, obviously not caring. "Rest, which is what you should be doing. Enjoy your wife's company."

Finn sighed, obviously annoyed that he had to spend a month in bed under Poppy's watchful eye.

"Do you remember what happened?"

"I was riding and then I remember falling; that's about it."

"A snake bit your horse's leg. It must have been hiding in the grass. Your horse got spooked and threw you off. You're lucky he didn't stomp you."

As soon as Hugh finished his checkup, Poppy came barreling in, holding a tray with tea, eggs, bacon, and toast.

She kept looking at him like a nervous rabbit, as if afraid he was going to die right then and there.

It would be a while before Poppy's nerves were settled, and Finn made a silent vow never to make her worry like this again.

Poppy's eyes watered when she put the food down.

"Breakfast."

"Thank you, sweetheart."

"Eat slow. The last thing you need is to throw it up. After breakfast, have Poppy draw you a bath and change the sheets. Or I could do it for you." He grinned, obviously joking.

"We'll be fine," Finn snapped. The last thing he needed was for his brother-in-law to see him naked, even though as his doctor, he had probably seen that and more while he was unconscious.

"Stop teasing him, Hugh. I am perfectly capable of drawing him a bath."

"Fine. I will leave you two lovebirds alone and I'll come check on you this afternoon before dinner. I'm sure my brothers would like to see you." Hugh left quickly, leaving them alone. Finally.

Poppy gave him a quick kiss on the forehead before she went downstairs and started hauling buckets of hot water up the stairs to fill the tub. He offered to help her, but he just received a glare in return.

"Here, let me help you." Poppy stood beside him, placing an arm around his torso and under his armpit to help him up.

"I can walk by myself, Pops."

"Nonsense. You've been unconscious for five days. You'll be lucky if you don't trip and fall."

That part was true at least. His legs felt numb, as if they belonged on a newborn calf.

"You're shaking," Finn pointed out once he finally managed to stand up. He forced himself to stand perfectly still so he didn't squish his much smaller wife. "Were you that afraid that something was going to happen to me?"

"You were unconscious for five days. I thought you were going to make me a widow before our first anniversary."

"Never. After waiting for you for so long, did you really think I was going to let you go?"

Poppy gave him a shaky smile. She looked like the one who needed to spend a few days in bed, not him.

Thankfully, they had a tub in a small room attached to their bedroom so Finn didn't have to go all the way downstairs.

"Easy now." Poppy helped him into the piping hot water. He let out a sigh of relief when his sore muscles were caressed by the warm water. He just hoped he would be able to move without whimpering in the next few days. He hated feeling like an invalid and Poppy wasn't strong enough to carry him.

"How does that feel?" Poppy bit her lower lip as if afraid he was going to lash out at her.

"Very nice." He tweaked her nose playfully. "Now, will you stop looking so scared?"

It was apparently the wrong thing to say because she burst into tears like a toddler. "Oh, Finn, I am so sorry!"

"Why are you apologizing?" he asked, startled.

"Because if we hadn't gotten into a fight, then I wouldn't have kicked you out and your horse wouldn't have been bitten," she blubbered as tears spilled down her cheeks.

"Oh, Pop, honey, it was an accident. Absolutely no one could have predicted this." He kissed her temple. "I'm not angry at you. I'm angry at myself for allowing Hugh to encourage me to do something so irrational. Perhaps my accident was my punishment for acting so foolishly. Now, no more tears," he said firmly, grasping her by her chin. "It wasn't anyone's fault. Let's just focus on the bath, all right?"

Poppy nodded somberly as she grabbed a rag and a bar of soap and started cleaning him. The touch from her sweet little hand only managed to get him uncomfortably hard. It took all his willpower not to ask her to get into the tub so she could ride him.

"I missed you," Poppy whispered as she continued bathing him. "A lot. I was afraid I was never going to see you again."

"Well, I'm here, Pop." He kissed the back of her hand. "I made a vow to you that I would be with you until death do us part and I intend to keep it."

The next few weeks were torturous for Finn in the sense that he hated being stuck in bed with Poppy fussing over him like a mother hen. He appreciated how much she worried over him, but he could barely use the outhouse without her trailing behind him like a little mouse.

"Let's go on a walk," Finn announced three weeks after his accident as he stood up from the breakfast table.

His wife gave him a panicked glance. "Now? But you're injured."

"I'm fine. Hugh cleared me yesterday. I return to work next week. I want to go on a walk with my wife, Poppy." Poppy frowned, obviously disagreeing. He placed a hand around her waist and started to drag her towards the front door.

Poppy sighed. "Fine. Let me get our coats first. It's chilly."

Once they were bundled up, they walked arm in arm around their property in silence, feeling the cold wind on their faces as Poppy snuggled against his chest. "This is nice," she finally admitted. "I hadn't realized how cooped up we had been."

"We both needed a break from your fussing," he teased her.

Poppy rolled her eyes. "Thanks to my fussing, you are alive and well."

Finn laughed, sneaking in a kiss. "I love you, Poppy Bennington Weston. Thank you for taking care of me."

Poppy rubbed her head against his chest. "You're welcome and I love you, Finn. Let's take care of each other from now on."

His lips were pressed against the side of her forehead. "Always."

Epilogue

"WE NEED TO GET UP, Finn. Stop kissing me!" Poppy complained as Finn pressed his lips against her neck and then toward the swell of her breasts. The fire was roaring happily in their bedroom, making it that much harder for them to get up, especially since they were both still naked underneath the covers.

Finn ignored his wife as his hand rested against her waist.

Poppy scowled as she slapped his hand away. "Stop it! We need to get ready. I promised Lucy I was going to help her with the Christmas breakfast. I won't be much help to her if I'm lying down in bed, will I?"

Lucy and Christopher had generously invited the entire family to the Bennington home to celebrate Christmas, as was tradition. Lucy was planning a festive Christmas breakfast feast while Steve and Ruby planned on bringing games for the kids to play with, even though Lloyd and Silver were still practically babies.

Finn gently nipped her shoulder blade. "You're helping me."

Poppy scoffed, rolling her eyes as she got out of bed. Finn watched in fascination as her naked ass gently bounced. Knowing that he wasn't going to convince his wife to come back to bed anytime soon, he got up.

"Do you want us to open our presents now or later?" Finn inquired. He had taken the train to Laramie earlier this week and had picked up a box full of hair accessories for his wife. Bows, ribbons, faux flowers, and feathers, along with other head pieces had filled the box completely. He hoped she would like them. He was nearly bursting in excitement at the thought of giving them to her.

Finn liked seeing her more confident and experimenting with bright colors and clothes instead of the dreary clothes she had worn after her mother's funeral. His wife seemed happier and he was going to stop at nothing to continue making her happy.

"I'll go first." Poppy picked up her robe that she had draped over one of their settees yesterday and covered up her nudity, much to his chagrin. She headed towards her wardrobe and pulled out a small box with a bright red bow on top.

Her hands were nearly trembling as she gave it to him. "Here. Merry Christmas, husband."

Finn pressed his lips against her temple. "Merry Christmas, wife."

He pulled apart the ribbon. It was something small. Perhaps it was a new comb, a scarf, or one of those fancy shaving tools from back east. Poppy always gave practical presents. She had always been a sensible woman.

Once he pulled the ribbon apart, he opened the box and pulled out a pair of yellow knitted booties. He swallowed. His brain froze as he stared at the baby booties again as if waiting for them to talk.

His wife was looking at him expectantly, with a big smile on her pretty face. "Do you like your gift?"

Finn felt like he was going to faint. "Pop, are you trying to tell me that you are with child?"

"Yes." She placed a hand on her belly. "At first, I didn't think much of it since I've never been very regular when it comes to my monthlies, and with the stress of your injuries, I wasn't thinking about dates." She blushed pink. "But when I noticed my breasts growing bigger and that I started gaining weight, I went to get checked out by a midwife and then by Hugh. Hugh says the baby will be born sometime in May. Are you happy?"

"Ecstatic. Thank you for giving me a lovely present. My own gift pales in comparison." Finn kissed her again, wrapping his arms around her. "Are you all right? Does anything hurt? I haven't been too rough with you, have I? Do you think we should get a maid? You shouldn't overexert yourself. What does Hugh think?"

Poppy laughed as she pressed a hand against his cheek. "I am perfectly fine, Finn. I'm expecting our son or daughter, something plenty of women have done before for centuries. I'll be all right as long as I have you constantly by my side."

"And you will." He draped a blanket around her shoulders. She rolled her eyes at the fussing but didn't complain. "Should we tell the family today, or would you like to wait?"

"We should tell them after breakfast," Poppy decided as she grabbed Finn's hand. "It will be a nice surprise for both of us to share."

"We're going to have a family." Finn grinned at her.

"We are already a family," Poppy whispered as she placed his hand on her belly. "We are just adding one more member."

Annabelle Marin

Annabelle Marin is a twenty-something romantic who lives in sunny California. When she isn't writing she enjoys daydreaming, watching way too much TV, and cuddling with her pets.

Her books are sweet erotic romances with domestic discipline. In her books you can expect: a spoonful of sweetness, a dash of sass, a cup of naughtiness, and an abundance of romance.

You can follow Annabelle on Facebook, Instagram, Goodreads, and Bookbub for exciting updates on upcoming books!

Facebook-https://www.facebook.com/annabelle.marin.940/
Instagram-https://www.instagram.com/
missannabellemarin/
Bookbub-//www.bookbub.com/profile/annabelle-marin
Goodreads-www.goodreads.com/author/show/21061973.
Annabelle_Marin

Don't miss these exciting titles by Annabelle Marin and Blushing Books!

Stand Alone Titles

Endless Paradise
Between Kisses & Lies

Letters to Holly
On the Dotted Line
His Southern Belle

Earthly Mates Series
The Alien's Mate

The Benningtons Series
Holy Matrimony
Strawberry Kiss

The Hollis Sisters Series
The Affair
The Scandal
The Passion

The Stevenson Brothers Series
The Rancher Orders a Bride
The Pastor Takes a Wife
The Sheriff Finds a Fiancée

Vintage Beauties Series

Bless Her Heart
Becoming a Gibson Girl
The Modern Housewife
Vintage Beauties Collection

The Bride Series

The Unwilling Mrs.
The Unattainable Bride
The Unexpected Wife

Anthologies

12 Naughty Days of Christmas 2021

Blushing Books

Blushing Books is one of the oldest eBook publishers on the web. We've been running websites that publish spanking and BDSM related romance and erotica since 1999, and we have been selling eBooks since 2003. We hope you'll check out our hundreds of offerings at http://www.blushingbooks.com.

Blushing Books Newsletter

Please join the Blushing Books newsletter
to receive updates & special promotional offers.
You can also join by using your mobile phone:
Just text BLUSHING to 22828.